Wictred's Fire

Wictred's Fire

ISBN 978-0-6151-7460-0

Chapter 1
The Northwood Games

In days long past, when the castle was the strongest defense known to man, there were nonetheless some activities that would be recognizable today. One of these was the Northwood Games.

"ARE YOU READY?" yelled the judge.

Frealaf locked eyes with Eadgils, the moneylender's son, who sat across from him on the other side of the table. This was the first round of the arm wrestling event. They were at the annual boys' strength and agility games of Northwood, the forest where Frealaf lived. This year the elders of the forest thought it would be interesting to bring in some children from Edlad, the capital city, to see how big city boys compared to the forest boys.

"You've got a tough one in first round," Frealaf's father Anlaf had told him. "Don't take him lightly."

"You must be kidding," Frealaf thought once he saw his opponent. Eadgils looked younger and smaller than himself. He probably spent most of his time reading, not chopping wood or shooting the bow and arrow like Frealaf. Besides, everyone knew that city kids were soft compared to forest kids. Frealaf's friend Aldhelm was here somewhere, and he had wanted to show Aldhelm that he could do well in the contest, but how could he against such weak competition?

Well, maybe this would be fun anyway. People like the moneylender may have money, they may have all the advantages, but there was one thing they could only dream about: toughness. All year long those people had their feet on the necks of the loggers, but at this time of year there could be a small measure of payback. Now they will see who the man is and who the little boy is, thought Frealaf.

Eadgils put his elbow up on the table and they locked hands. This year Frealaf would bring home the trophy to his sick little brother Odanae. This year the other Northwood kids would move out of the way when he walked by. This year . . .

"Go!" yelled the judge. Sweat poured and muscles trembled.

But almost before Frealaf knew it, he felt the humiliating bite of wood on the back of his hand. Eadgils had beaten him.

"The winner!" yelled the judge as he raised Eadgils' arm.

A few groans were heard coming from several Northwood boys who had been watching.

"I thought you forest kids were supposed to be tough," said Eadgils contemptuously.

Frealaf felt his face going red. He stepped down from the table in a daze, went over to the sidelines, and sat down. He was surprised by a hand on his shoulder.

"Don't worry, *son*, there's always next year," said Eadgils right before he slapped Frealaf on the cheek so hard his eyes teared up.

Frealaf wheeled around to throw a punch at Eadgils, but a judge caught his hand.

"None of that! We'll have none of that here," said the judge.

Who the man is and who the little boy is. But his opponent was obviously a little boy. Did that mean that he was a . . .

"Did you make him look bad?" laughed Aldhelm from behind.

BAM! Frealaf turned and hit Aldhelm on the side of the face.

Aldhelm hit Frealaf in the chest and sent him staggering backwards. Several judges came charging in and broke them up.

"All right, all right," said one of the judges, "you're both out of here. Get!"

And with that both Frealaf and Aldhelm were disqualified from further competition.

Frealaf didn't realize that Aldhelm had not seen his match, and had assumed he had won.

The two friends did not talk to each other again that day. Anlaf loaded them on to the wagon, where they both sat in silence the whole way back home. After a ride of several hours, Anlaf dropped off Aldhelm at his father Forthred's house. A mile and a half later Anlaf arrived at his own house. Gudlaug, Anlaf's wife, noticed that her son was unusually quiet.

After an athletic event he was usually very vocal. Frealaf walked past Odanae's room, plopped down in the chair and closed his eyes.

"How did your match go?" Anlaf's voice interrupted Frealaf's thoughts.

"Uh . . ." Frealaf could not react to his father the way he had to Aldhelm, nor could he avoid the question. He hung his head.

"Uh . . . I lost," he said.

"Well, let me tell you something you might be interested in. Your opponent's elbow left the table, and the judges didn't call it," said Anlaf.

"He cheated?" said Frealaf, lifting his head. "But how did you know?"

"I was watching," said Anlaf.

"I didn't see you. How come you didn't say anything?" he asked.

"You weren't wrestling the way I taught you," said Anlaf. "Didn't I tell you not to underestimate your opponent? To be aware of your surroundings? -- You just closed your eyes once the judge said go. Then you got angry. Don't you know the judges are the moneylender's friends? We sure don't need any more trouble with him."

When King Athelgar was in Kara Mundalyn, he had considered these games so important that he sponsored and regulated them. But several years ago he rode East with his army and failed to return. He left behind a lovely daughter, princess Erinndis, who became Queen after hopes for Athelgar's return had faded, and she took no interest in the games.

This lack of royal oversight meant that impartial judges were a thing of the past. Now their decisions were biased in favor of whoever had the most power or money.

"Why didn't you tell me he cheated on the way back?" said Frealaf.

"Aldhelm would have heard, and he might have told his father. And you know Forthred . . . he might have ridden back to the games to break some arms. Or even worse . . . he might have told his uncle Cnebba.

9

And nobody needs *that* kind of trouble," said Anlaf, shaking his head.

The next morning, Aldhelm appeared at Frealaf's front door.

"Dad's away buying some saws," said Aldhelm. "Do you want to go out to the pond? I've got something to show you."

"Sorry I . . ." started Frealaf.

"No big problem," said Aldhelm. "Forget it."

"Well, my dad is here but he gave me the day off. I'll be right out," said Frealaf.

After they arrived at the pond, there didn't appear to be anything that wasn't there the last time they visited.

"Okay, where is it?" asked Frealaf.

"Right here," said Aldhelm, grabbing his friend.

Frealaf found himself flying through the air into the water, from which he came up sputtering and laughing. Any bad feelings between Frealaf and Aldhelm had ended.

Still it did not end the hostilities between Frealaf and Eadgils, for the Northwood games was not the last time those two would meet.

. . .

After hopes for Athelgar's return had faded,

10

Erinndis began to feel so chilled that she couldn't warm herself up. No matter how many blankets she piled on or how high the fire was stoked, she continued to shiver. Her chill turned out to be the beginning of an affliction which no physician could cure.

The disease did not go away when springtime came. The terrible sickness agonized her body and twisted her countenance. She began to look much older than her tender years. Soon after she became the Queen, her appearance had been so affected that her subjects feared to behold her. Some said that the Queen was now as ugly as one of the river-horses of the far South. No one in the kingdom had ever seen these river-horses, but everyone seemed to know how terribly ugly they were.

One evening Erinndis was in particularly great distress. Then Adrastos the priest brought the Emerald of Healing from its vault and took it to the Queen's bedroom. The Emerald was carried about in a little wooden box. The box was covered with a red velvet blanket decorated with green vines bearing gold and silver berries.

Two of the priest's assistants stood at the foot of the Erinndis' bed and unveiled the Emerald, raising its blanket just enough so that she could see the Emerald. The Queen's face bathed in green light, and she was soon restored to health and beauty.

But this healing lasted only for the night; once the sunlight began to brighten the East, the Queen returned to her diseased condition. Even the Great Emerald could not totally break the power of whatever curse was upon her.

The pain of becoming sick again was so great that Erinndis had never asked for the Emerald again.

Chapter 2
Easy Lessons

The Proctor, so named for his time as chief examiner in Edlad, was dressed in a black coat and a black hat that covered his bald head. He had a great white beard that came half way down to his belt. The boys were fortunate to have such traveled tutor. The Proctor had once been ambassador to the land of Snagov and had met king Wictred himself. He knew first hand the evil that Wictred was capable of. He knew that such evil flourished most easily where people were ignorant. And he had dedicated his life to educating those young people in Kara Mundalyn who had no access to schools in the city.

"Time for your history lesson, young man," said the Proctor to Aldhelm and Frealaf.

Although both boys were present, the Proctor was speaking to Aldhelm in particular because he had more trouble paying attention to lessons than Frealaf did. Forthred had brought his son to Anlaf's house for the lesson, and both men sat in the kitchen while lessons proceeded in the living room. The Proctor opened an old black leather scroll and began to read.

"'In the days of old, before ever there was a king in the land . . .'"

Aldhelm was already looking out the window.

"Look here!" yelled the Proctor, snapping the boy back to attention.

"Your father does not pay me to sing you to sleep. Though he cannot read, he told me that you will learn . . . or else."

The Proctor pulled a wooden stick out of his cloak, and from here on in Aldhelm knew that if he dozed off, he would feel the hard rap of wood on his hand.

"'The terror that stalked by night, full of malice, even the great Ghoul . . .'"

Neither of the boys liked hearing about this subject, but it was considered essential to learning the history of the kingdom.

"' . . . was slain by the mighty Ealdulf the Bold; who laid it to rest under the Black Crag, far to the East of the Great Mountains that circle our kingdom. And he founded Kara Mundalyn in the land between the mountains'" said the Proctor.

"Those boys will surely read and write, as sure as water is wet," said Anlaf to Forthred. "If I could read well, that moneylender would surely not have been able to fool me the way he did."

"I know. I borrowed five silvers from him two years ago, and have paid him ten silvers since, yet he says I now owe him fifteen silvers. How could that be? He better not send his collectors to me, or I'll show them this," said Forthred, fingering his axe.

"'. . . and those who dug in the roots of the mountains'" continued the Proctor, "'found rare jewels: diamonds, sapphires, and emeralds, even the Emerald of Healing, the greatest of all gems ever unearthed by man: The Fire of Edlad. A priesthood was founded to guard the Emerald and all the gems of healing, that if any be gravely ill, they may bring forth the jewels to restore a life that would be cut short . . .'"

"I see why my son falls asleep," said Forthred.

"Yes, but don't tell the Proctor," whispered Anlaf.

They chuckled.

"AWAKE!" yelled the Proctor.

"Ouch!" complained Aldhelm, his wrist hurting from a rap of the teacher's stick.

Anlaf and Forthred also jumped a little at this outburst, even though they had seen it before.

"I'll nudge you," whispered Frealaf to Aldhelm.

"Silence! I will have silence," demanded the Proctor before continuing.

"Eadwacer and his cronies have a lock on just about all the wealth of Northwood. It has been a good many years since I've last talked to any Northwood lumberjacks who don't owe him money . . ." said Anlaf.

"And the worst thing is," Forthred broke in, "somehow he gets . . . what are they called? Titles or something, rights to the land, that our fathers hacked and carved out of the woods with their own might. He hasn't lifted a finger but he says he owns the land. Something has to be done!"

"'. . . then did Ealdulf send explorers, the bravest men in the land, to climb the great mountain in the center of the land. None could reach the top, and all who dared climb higher than the Face in the Rock died. But they did not give up, and so Ealdulf named it Mount Hope. He founded Edlad at its foot.'"

"Let us take care not to do anything that would cause the might of the kingdom to come against us," said Anlaf. "Though thieves now sit in high places, I am sure that the Queen and her advisors are not aware . . ."

"We need justice *now!*" interrupted Forthred, banging his fist on the table.

"With all due respect . . ." started the Proctor from the other room.

"Sorry," said Anlaf to the Proctor. "Let's take

this outside," he said to Forthred.

With that, Anlaf and Forthred left the house, and the Proctor continued his lesson.

"'And so it was prophesied that no evil shall ever set foot in Edlad as long as a scion of Ealdulf sits on the throne.' That concludes today's reading."

The Proctor closed the book.

"Now, boys, I want to see if you remember what you learned earlier. What lies east of the Black Crag, and what foul religion is practiced there?"

"The land of Snagov, and the Gthonic Mysteries!" said Frealaf.

"I know *you* know. Now let Aldhelm answer the next question. What two roads come in to the great gate of Edlad?"

"Uh . . . the road from the farmlands?" said Aldhelm.

"And?" said the Proctor.

"The . . . road from the ledge of Mount Hope.

"Very good, Aldhelm. I see you've been studying, at least some," said the Proctor.

Aldhelm had not been studying the way the Proctor thought, but because the boy was interested in exploring new places he had spied out this information on his last visit to Edlad. The next day they were planning to leave for another such visit.

Anlaf and Forthred were now talking politics loudly enough to be heard from outside.

"Its time to end this lesson. You have to get ready for your trip tomorrow. And from the sound of it we'd better get out there before your fathers tear the barn down."

After they went outside, the Proctor mounted his horse, Forthred loaded Aldhelm into the wagon, and all said their goodbyes.

Chapter 3
First Trip to Edlad

The next day Anlaf and Forthred loaded up their wagons with the very best timber, while Gudlaug prepared a bedroom for Beonoc and Caelin, hardy loggers who helped guard the homestead whenever Anlaf was gone. With the dogs barking and carrying on they began the journey to Edlad to supply the craftsmen there with wood.

On the last trip, Odanae had gone with them. He liked Edlad's great stone walls and castles. Every time he saw the towers of the city gleaming in the sun, his heart beat a little faster.

His artistic eye had pored over every detail of the structures, memorizing each nook and cranny. He would dream of the city long after they had left it. He could draw accurate pictures of the city from memory, and he also drew plans for new buildings that did not yet exist.

"One day I will build mighty walls like these," Odanae would think to himself.

"That wall would make a good place for target practice," thought Frealaf.

"I wonder what's on the other side of those walls," Aldhelm would think.

Today another such trip was underway, but Odanae was too sick to go, so only Frealaf and Aldhelm got into the wagons with their fathers. The wagons creaked and bumped along the rocky forest roads, logs bumping in back. The leaves rustled as mid morning wind sighed through the tree leaves. The broad canopy of green at the top of the forest blocked the sun for the most part but let some trickles of light through. Woodland animals hid as the noisy company made its way to the edge of the trees.

"Looks like the fields are growing nicely this year," said Forthred as they broke into the bright sunlight. "Two more months and harvest time will be here."

The rolling hills were checkered with farmers' fields for miles and miles, and though the wagons now rolled more quickly, the sun passed over and evening time came before they were near Edlad. Anlaf, Forthred and their boys made camp in the midst of the farmlands that night. The next day they broke camp at dawn and arrived in Edlad shortly after noon.

Forthred and Anlaf delivered their lumber to the craftsmen . . . the wheel makers received elm, oak, and ash; elm for the hubs, oak for the spokes, and ash for the rims. The cabinet and bed makers received mostly oak and walnut.

While the wagons were unloading the horses were watered and rested in the stables. At days end they all checked in to the Inn for rest and refreshment.

"We'll show you boys some of the night life of Edlad," said Anlaf and Forthred.

"Night life" in Edlad was not associated with a life of sloth and drunkenness as it was in other kingdoms. The Lumbermen were not taking their sons where they should not go. But there were risks. Some unsavory characters did frequent the pubs at night, even in Edlad.

"If that moneylender is in there, I don't want you to talk to him," whispered Anlaf to Frealaf.

Several years ago Eadwacer the moneylender had taken an interest in Odanae on one of Anlaf's trips to Edlad. Anlaf didn't mind at first, but two things changed his mind. First, he found out that Eadwacer had been cheating the lumberjacks. Second, after returning home, Odanae started waking up scared at night.

Gudlaug had talked with Odanae and discovered that the moneylender had given him a tiny carved image of a man, and told him that if he asked it a question before going to sleep and put it under his pillow, it would give an answer in his dreams.

Such talismans had been popular with young people in the kingdom for a number of years. Anlaf suspected they were being smuggled into the kingdom by people connected with the sorceress who lived in the woods at the foot of the mountains. Anlaf reasoned that anything coming from her couldn't be good, so he burned the carving and forbad his sons to talk with Eadwacer.

Torch lights flickered in the windows of the wooden pub, which seemed to grow larger as the lumberjacks walked toward it.

Tonight, however, the usual music and laughter were not in evidence. Instead they had walked in on some kind of community meeting, and it was not going particularly smoothly. Two factions composed of both men and boys were having some sort of disagreement.

"We can't just sit back and let them keep robbing our caravans," shouted one man. "We have to *do* something!"

"No!" yelled another. "We must wait for the Queen's troops to catch the bandits! Otherwise, how are we better than they?"

"Where's the ale?" whispered Forthred to the barrel keeper.

"Not tonight," said the barrel keeper. "Ale poured on this fire could burn this whole place down."

"We're losing money!" shouted the first man. "Why must we submit to the incursions of rogues from Snagov near our borders just because the Queen doesn't seem to think there's a problem?"

"You hold your tongue about the Queen," a yell came from the other side of the pub.

Anlaf noticed that the men who seemed to more or less favor the Queen appeared somewhat wealthier than those less favorably disposed toward her. Forthred continued trolling for refreshments, oblivious to his surroundings (as he often was) while Anlaf was absorbed in the proceedings at hand.

One of the less wealthy looking men jumped up on a table, roaring in a loud voice,

"You that have money can just wait out the hard times! But what about us? We go under!"

There was a rumble of approval from his side of the room.

"Look at those boys across the room," said Aldhelm to Frealaf. "Looks like they're getting ready to fight."

And sure enough, the younger men on both sides of the room were fidgeting and some of them were fiddling with things in their pockets, which Frealaf took to be weapons of some sort. Frealaf pulled at his father's coat, but Anlaf was totally absorbed in what the men were saying. Forthred was nowhere to be seen.

Shouts and yells continued to escalate until even Anlaf thought it was time to leave. But he would not leave without Forthred.

"You boys go outside and wait for us," he said as he went to look for Forthred.

As Aldhelm and Frealaf started making their way to the door, several men pushed over a table and the fight was on.

As luck would have it, Aldhelm and Frealaf were nearer to the wealthier looking faction, and looking as they did like boys from the poorer side of town, they were immediately set upon by about five boys their own age.

Frealaf was jumped on by three of the wealthy boys. The next thing he knew one of them was on top of him, preparing to pummel him in the face, but the men were fighting too, and one of them stumbled through the boys, knocking the other boy off of Frealaf. Frealaf tried to stand but was tripped up again. This time several of the wealthy boys jumped on top of him, but just then Aldhelm grabbed both of their collars and hauled them off backward.

The other three boys then jumped on Aldhelm. Frealaf, still down, grabbed at one of Aldhelm's attackers foot, tripping him. As Frealaf struggled to his feet, other poorer boys came in and evened the odds. Eyes were blackened as fists swung.

"Watch me take that forest boy," said a voice.

As Frealaf turned to see who spoke, someone hit him in the eye and then yanked his neck down in a headlock. Then Frealaf remembered the voice. It was Eadgils the moneylender's son.

Stunned, he found himself staggering around. Every time he tried to set his feet, Eadgils was already pulling him off balance in another direction.

Frealaf could tell he was slowly being maneuvered in a particular direction. Then he felt himself being thrown down, with Eadgils landing on top of him. He had been pulled in to a side room of the pub, and someone closed the door.

Inside the room were several wealthier looking kids, evidently Eadgils' friends. So that was it . . . Eadgils had taken Frealaf into the room so he could torment him in front of his friends.

Eadgils straddled Frealaf's stomach as if to start punching him in the face.

Why fight back, thought Frealaf. There are too many of them, and I can't even beat one of them. He prepared for a beating, and went limp.

But Eadgils was not even going to allow Frealaf the dignity of getting beaten up. Instead of punching, he casually lowered his palm and pressed it down on Frealaf's nose. Frealaf felt tears welling up.

"What's the matter? Going to cry, Freylaug?" said Eadgils.

"Freylaug?" he thought. "That's a girl's name!"

Something broke within Frealaf. This was going too far. It no longer mattered whether he won or lost, he had to fight this. Enraged, he wrapped his legs around Eadgils' head and arms and threw him off.

25

Both boys got back on their feet and began to grapple. It was then that Frealaf noticed that Eadgils, though strong for a city boy, was not quite as powerful as he was himself. So he threw Eadgils to the ground, got on top of him, and began to hit him. The other kids in the room were not brave enough to intervene, and Frealaf was on the verge of pummeling Eadgils to a pulp when Anlaf and Forthred came crashing through the door. They had already grabbed Aldhelm and now they also took Frealaf, dragging both of them toward the door.

"This isn't over yet, forest boy!" Eadgils half cried, half yelled at Frealaf.

"Why in the world is that boy so mad? What have I ever done to him except defend myself?" thought Frealaf. He resolved to wrestle Aldhelm every day from now on to prepare himself for his next meeting with Eadgils.

"I thought you were going to kill the lot of them," chuckled Anlaf to his son. "I had to come in and save them!"

Frealaf liked the sound of that, but he was also glad his father did not know what had happened behind the closed door . . . that for a moment he had been willing to let Eadgils beat on him. Frealaf vowed that never again would he ever, ever give in to a bully that easily.

The way Anlaf was laughing and carrying on with Forthred, it seemed as if both of them had thoroughly enjoyed the night's proceedings.

The boys didn't understand what all the talk in the pub had been about. Their fathers didn't either, but they understood a great deal more than their sons.

They understood that raiders from Snagov were taking a great toll on the merchants of Kara Mundalyn. They understood that these raids were occurring on trade routes right on the border of the country, outside the Great Mountains. And they understood that the Queen and her advisors were taking a cautious approach to the problem, only sending out small sorties to chase these raiders, and that more raiders kept on showing up.

The wealthier merchants preferred a wait and see approach for the time being, and the ones who were losing their livelihoods wanted to form posses to go out and try to deal with the problem themselves.

Finally, they were all back in their room at the Inn.

The boys looked at each other and smiled, for both of them had bumps and bruises . . . badges of honor.

"Let that be a lesson to you," said Forthred to the boys. "Never accompany two ignorant lumberjacks to the city at night!"

"Hmmph," said Anlaf, who was already falling asleep on his bed.

Frealaf slept better that night than he could remember ever having done.

Chapter 4
The Royal Council

Erinndis looked out the window of the king's royal castle, from where she had ruled since she became Queen two years ago. She knew there were problems in the kingdom, but she had faith in Adrastos the Priest, who was her regent, helping her rule until she got older.

She later remembered this day because the most beautiful white dove she had ever seen flew by her window. Its wings beat with the softest, sweetest whipping sound, and every time its wings beat the dove peeped softly. Queen Erinndis felt her heart soar with the dove, and for a moment she felt good again, as she had before her father left.

The sun was nearing its pinnacle in the bright blue above, and she looked East out over the stone houses nestled in and around the green trees that populated that part of the city. When she looked West, she could see fewer trees, but many shops in the marketplace, all bustling with people coming in and out. A stream that flowed into the city under the walls from the East and out of the walls to the West connected the residential section with the market.

She looked back up at the expanse of the heavens. The golden light of the sun turned the edges of the few clouds into jewels most precious, and when it emerged from behind them, the stream winding through the middle of the capitol answered the sky with its own sparkling lights.

"Light is sweet," she thought, and then she reluctantly left the window and turned her attention to the more mundane matters of learning to run the kingdom.

The meeting convened in Great Hall of the Royal Castle. The Hall was made of strong stone walls and had great wooden beams supporting its ceiling. On the Northern side hung a great curtain emblazoned with the Royal Emblems of the House of Knight – red shields decorated with golden lions and crossed silver swords. During the daytime the sun streamed in the arched windows and the Royal Emblems shone brightly (at night the Hall was quite a bit gloomier). A great wooden table stood in the center of the Hall, where in former times the Kings of Kara Mundalyn would hold important meetings. Adrastos thought it good to continue this tradition, and so the Queen held her meetings there as well.

The most important people scheduled to be in attendance were the two priests, Adrastos and Skaldar; Lord Sigeric of the Southern March, Healfdene the chief of the guards, Heorogar the Strong, who was the greatest of the Knights that had remained behind when Athelgar rode forth; and a few thanes of lesser importance. All told there were about twenty people in attendance.

Queen Erinndis officially presided over the meeting, but as she was still young, said nothing. She preferred instead to learn in silence while Adrastos taught by example how to hold such a meeting. All stood round the table while the Queen sat, then all who have been named sat except Adrastos the priest (the thanes and servants did not sit at all but went to stand near the doors). Adrastos began the meeting with the traditional invocation and greeting.

"I greet you all in the name of the Most High King, whose dwelling is not with men," said Adrastos in a loud voice. "May He be honored forever."

"So be it," said all in the room.

After a brief pause, Adrastos continued. "The meeting will come to order. The first item to be discussed is that of defense and fortifications. Heorogar?"

Heorogar stood and Adrastos sat.

"My Queen," he said as he bowed in her direction, "and noble members of the council," he said as he nodded in theirs, "our fortresses are in need of repair in some places, but most of them are still strong. Our army continues to be strong. We have about forty thousand men ready to fight on foot, and about ten thousand archers who can hit a man at 180 paces. And," he said with chest swelling a bit, "twenty five thousand knights ready to ride at a minute's notice."

"What about training?" said Adrastos. "Are the younger men prepared for battle?"

"Those under forty years of age have never seen a large battle, but then, there haven't been any. There have been many instances of marauders outside of the mountains, who often raid the merchant's caravans. We like to send our trainees with the older soldiers to go out and skirmish with them, but there have been no engagements involving more than a few dozen men at a time. These raids are on the increase and we may soon be forced to take stronger action."

Those present were beginning to digest this information, when Heorogar chuckled and blurted out rather undiplomatically,

"Thank God for those marauders, or the trainees wouldn't have seen any action at all!"

"All right, all right" said Adrastos, who was not overly amused at the invocation of the Almighty to make such a point, though he did not say so outright. "What has intelligence gathered?"

The exact methods of intelligence gathering were not discussed in open meetings. Since there were some servants present whose loyalty had been sworn but not tested under battle conditions, all unproven people were dismissed at this point. After they quietly shuffled out of the room, the meeting continued.

"We think," said Heorogar, "that the Gthonic warriors of Snagov are again on the march. Several large castles between the land of Snagov and Kara Mundalyn have been besieged, and many large companies of Gthonic knights have been sighted in places where they don't usually go, in lands barely one hundred miles from the Great Mountains. However, we don't have any idea what they are up to, and as yet their professional soldiers have made no move to approach Kara Mundalyn. I might add that our merchants are none to happy with the losses they suffer from the Gthonic marauders."

"Our policy for the present time is to allow them restricted access to the areas just outside our borders, so we can keep an eye on them," said Adrastos.

"I think that we need to meet them with more force," said Heorogar.

"Heorogar is right," said a suddenly animated Healfdene. "Where Gthonic raiders are, Gthonic invaders can't be far behind. Their presence reeks with the stench of Wictred the Vengeful."

King Wictred the Vengeful, so called ever since he settled a gambling debt to his brother with a sword in the back, had a history of sending out feeler sorties before attacking with force. Several voices grunted in approval of Healfdene's words.

"Yet, the actions of these marauders are our best weathervane to tell us which way the political winds in the land of Snagov are blowing, for in the past Gthonic incursions have often increased right before a Gthonic invasion. Unfortunately, we must not tell the merchants this; otherwise, word may get back to the land of Snagov and they may take more care to hide their actions," said Adrastos.

Adrastos paused and sighed, as if he did not like the sound his own words.

"Perhaps we can release some of the funds of the treasury to compensate our suffering merchants for some of their losses. At any rate must keep unsleeping vigilance, but other than that, there is nothing more to be done for the present moment," concluded Adrastos.

Although those present were not in total agreement with this cautious approach, they held their peace for the time being, and the meeting continued.

"My Queen, and noble members of the council," said Healfdene, "the country remains mostly at peace. We have one hundred fifty tithings of men (i.e., fifteen thousand) patrolling the kingdom. At this time half of them are in Edlad, the other half are in other parts of the kingdom. There have been some major robberies in the city but as we speak the ringleaders are in prison waiting for judgment."

"And the royal guard?" asked Adrastos.

"Two thousand of your majesty's most skilled troops, five hundred of which are ready to fight immediately, the rest within ten minutes," said Healfdene.

"Thank you, Healfdene," said Adrastos. "Until we better understand the forces at work on our borders, it is best to keep ourselves ready for war at all times."

And so it went . . . military men discussing the

army, priests discussing the piety of the kingdom, and merchants being called in to discuss economic issues. All in all, the kingdom was prospering, despite the losses of those who invested in foreign trade to raiders on the border.

All those scheduled to be there were present, except for Skaldar the priest, who had been excused due to ill health.

For the most part the meeting went well, and the Queen left it with renewed admiration at the way that Adrastos had presided over it. She had learned much and almost felt she could run such a meeting herself. But now that the excitement of the meeting was over, the pain that was always with her seemed to get worse.

It was mid afternoon when the meeting adjourned, and the sun still bathed Edlad in its beautiful light. Erinndis sought refuge on the high tower of the royal castle, a place where she could again gaze at the beauty of the city and perhaps to see the dove. The dove did not return.

That night, when the affairs of the day were over and Queen Erinndis was alone in her bedroom, she felt miserably cold and her back and knees ached terribly. She hoped that sleep would make her forget her pain for a while, until tomorrow when perhaps a walk in the Orchard would also make her feel better. This hope would be realized. However, some seemingly small happenings beginning in another forest foreshadowed events that would make her feel much, much worse.

Chapter 5
A Visit to the Depths

Adrastos' knees ached as he descended a long flight of steep stone stairs. His footsteps echoed off of the narrowing stone walls. He was going to visit Skaldar, whose illness caused him to shun sunlight, favoring instead the recesses beneath the castle. As he went lower it became so dark that he had to light a torch to continue. Finally he arrived at the bottom of the stairs, where the stone walls broadened out into a little room that looked even more ancient than those parts of the castle that were above ground. Spider webs seemed to have claimed the corners and moisture clung to the rocky walls at this cold depth.

There were two creaky wooden doors at the bottom facing the stairs. The one on the left had a large iron lock on it. The one on the right was Skaldar's.

Adrastos knocked and entered; the room was

sparsely furnished, with one bed in one corner, the fireplace in the middle and a chair and table in the opposite corner. Skaldar had pulled the chair in front of the fireplace, and was boiling something in a big black pot when Adrastos entered. Adrastos' nose twitched slightly. He knew much about the pharmaceutical sciences, but he did not recognize the brew that his colleague had made.

"Greetings, my friend," said Skaldar. "As always, it is good to see your face." Skaldar looked bent and old, and his eyes were slightly glazed.

"Greetings in the name of the Most High King, whose dwelling is not with men," said Adrastos.

"Right," said Skaldar.

From the dead tone in Skaldar's voice, Adrastos inferred that there was more wrong with him than he thought, for priests were usually more enthusiastic when speaking of the Lord. He resolved to pray for him even more fervently.

"I brought you some bread," said Adrastos.

"Thank you. Put it on the table," said Skaldar.

"How are you today?" said Adrastos.

"The pain has been hard on me today. Almost time for my . . . medicine . . ." said Skaldar, leaning over the pot.

The pot bubbled with little popping sounds, and occasionally a little bit of the brew would spill into the fire, hissing when it hit.   Adrastos noticed that the spiders had claimed the corners of this room as well.

"How is the translation coming?" said Adrastos.

"Actually, the translation is coming quite well," said Skaldar, eyes brightening considerably.   "You would be amazed at the way that people lived back then.   They had such remarkable, uh, science and learning . . . I would have to say that in important ways they were more advanced than we are."

"Have you constructed a timeline for their history yet? Have you been able to assign a date to the scroll?" said Adrastos.

"Well, there was not as much history as we had first thought," said Skaldar, eyes distant with thought. "The scroll is old, but I'm not certain how old."

"It certainly looked like history from our initial reading of it," said Adrastos.

"It turned out the historical terminology appeared only in the prolegomenon," replied Skaldar. "And despite the historical form of writing, I'm not sure that it is to be taken literally. The rest of the text deals strictly with the art and science of the time."

"And the spells.   Do you have any trouble skipping over them, or are they woven into the text so tightly that you must read some of them?" asked Adrastos.

"I've learned to identify them so quickly that my eyes are averted almost before I am aware of them," replied Skaldar.

"Tell me more about the arts and science of those days. If the history is lacking, maybe we can deduce some of it from what we do have," said Adrastos.

Skaldar's eyes glazed over again.

"Perhaps some other time," he said, sounding suddenly weary. "My strength is still not what is should be."

Adrastos had the nagging feeling that Skaldar's weariness was due more to a desire to avoid discussing the historical aspects of the scroll than it was due to disease. Nevertheless there was nothing more to be done now other than to begin the long trek back up the stairs.

Chapter 6
Some Strange Happenings

"Ready?" said Frealaf.

"Ready," said Aldhelm.

Frealaf dove at Aldhelm's legs to take him down; Aldhelm shot his legs back and wrapped his arms around Frealaf's ribcage, and the fight was on. But it was a friendly match. Frealaf was serious about getting in better shape in case he had to fight again, and Aldhelm, bigger than Frealaf, was all too happy to oblige. Frealaf lost this match, but every time out he was getting tougher and tougher. Once in a while Forthred would stop by and give the boys some tips.

Today they were visiting Forthred's uncle Cnebba to pick up a load of wood. Cnebba was on even worse terms with the moneylender than Forthred, for he had killed some of the moneylender's collectors who tried to take by force some gold that Forthred didn't owe. After that he had moved to a remote location in the woods where he couldn't be found.

After their workout, the boys went into the house for a drink while Forthred prepared the wagon to receive its load.

Cnebba could not hear the boys unless they shouted at him, which they greatly enjoyed doing.

"Old Burgleburper really likes to chase them rabbits," said Cnebba, patting the head of a large dog under the table. "Can't catch em, but he chased the one to me that you're eatin now."

Frealaf put his hand on his mouth to hide a smile.

"Burgle-Burper?" said Aldhelm with a raised eyebrow.

"Huh?" said Cnebba.

"BURGLEBURPER?" yelled Aldhelm.

"Yep, he burps like a baby after eatin a burglar" said Cnebba.

Frealaf's shoulders shook as he tried to stifle his laughter.

"You think that's funny? Just look at the fangs on this monster," said Cnebba, fumbling with the big dog's ample lips, which produced plenty of saliva, but as far as the boys could tell, no teeth at all.

"Slobberlips would have been a better name for that thing," said Aldhelm.

"*Huh?*" yelled Cnebba, straining to hear. "I been namin dogs since before both your daddies was born, and now you think you know more about dog namin' than me?" he growled.

Both boys now lost control and burst out laughing.

"Bah!" Barked Cnebba, and he got up rapidly, knocking over his chair.

Now when Cnebba's chair fell over as he got up, that usually meant he was getting agitated, which was sometimes bad for anyone close to him, so the boys ran out the door.

"You two better stop bothering uncle Cnebba, or he might forget you're boys and take you for squawking chickens," said Forthred. "Cook you and eat you, he will."

Aldhelm and Frealaf might have been terrified five years ago at such a threat, but now they weren't much worried. Nevertheless, neither of them ventured back into the house until evening when Forthred went in for dinner.

Finally, it was time to leave, so Forthred loaded up the wagon and took off toward home. When they returned to their own country, Forthred took Frealaf home and then continued on to his own house.

That night, as Frealaf lay in bed, he could overhear parts of a conversation between his mom and dad.

"I tell you, there was no plan! I had no idea that boy from the tournament was going to be there," said dad.

"It's just that I don't want you teaching our son to fight," said mom.

"Teach him? He already knows. You should have seen the way he . . ."

"Anlaf!" said mom.

The next afternoon, Aldhelm and Frealaf were spending some time skipping stones across the pond in the woods. The boys were aiming at a round rock that poked its head up out of the water in the middle of the pond. They often aimed at it, since it was not easy to hit, but once in a while one of their stones would bounce off of it.

"You have to get the right shape for your stone, and throw it like this . . ," Aldhelm would tell his friend.

Aldhelm had a very strong arm and could make his stones skip many times, sometimes as many as six; and he was the only boy who had ever hit the target. Frealaf could barely manage three of four skips.

On this particular day, however, one of Frealaf's stones skipped five times. On the fifth skip, however, it went off at a funny angle, slowed, and hit the target rock; not bouncing off of it, but landing perfectly on top of it.

"Wow!" said Aldhelm. "I guess you're the champion now."

Aldhelm tried several times to match his friend's throw, and although he had some good tries, nothing could come close to Frealaf's accomplishment.

"You'd better swim out and get your stone," said Aldhelm. "It is a lucky stone."

Frealaf thought for a moment.

"No, I don't think so."

"Why not?" said Aldhelm.

"Well . . ."

"Well what?"

"Maybe it was meant to stay there," said Frealaf.

"What??" said Aldhelm.

Frealaf had the feeling that his throw was just a little bit odd. It had seemed to him as if something had altered the direction of his stone. He did not want to admit any fear to Aldhelm, but neither did wish to enter the water under such circumstances.

"Maybe it was *meant* to stay there," repeated Frealaf.

"What kind of stupid do you have to be to think that?" said Aldhelm. "Does a stone have a reason for falling the way it does? You should be glad you have me to look out for you, otherwise you would surely blunder yourself to death," said Aldhelm, laughing.

Frealaf laughed also, for he knew his friend's words were not meant to hurt, at least not too much. The good cheer lightened his mood, but something still didn't feel right to Frealaf. Maybe it was just the lengthening shadows of approaching evening. Getting lost in the forest was a real threat, for they were miles from home.

"We'd better get going," said Frealaf.

"Yeah," agreed Aldhelm.

They picked up their bows (all forest boys carried weapons in those days) and set off toward home. Aldhelm's home was a mile closer to the pond than Frealaf's, so they said goodbye and Aldhelm turned off the path toward his father's stone cabin.

Frealaf walked a lonely road for that last mile, and right after his friend was out of earshot his earlier uneasiness returned with a vengeance. He kept looking behind him. Do you know the feeling that someone is there, but you can't see anyone? Frealaf kept having the feeling that someone was following him in the lengthening shadows. Several times he fingered an arrow into his bow, for he was a crack shot and could hit anything that moved. But this evening, every time he looked for a target he could never find one. Finally he heard a twig snap, and he broke into a run.

· · ·

Anlaf was strong as a forest oak, but not as young as he used to be, and today his back hurt. So after moving lumber in the morning, he quit in the afternoon and went home to rest.

"Don't have to kill myself every day," he thought.

After he walked in to his cabin, he went in to say hello to Gudlaug, who was boiling a huge pot of food in the fireplace.

"Hello, my dear," said he, and they greeted each other happily. He grabbed a brand from the fire to light a candle by the front door, which was his custom whenever Frealaf was out late. The light in the doorway meant "come on in." The candle would be extinguished when the whole family was together and the doors were locked. Anlaf went to rest in his chair, but it was gone.

"I moved it outside so the sun could freshen it," said Gudlaug, and Anlaf went back to the front door. The candle was out.

Wind must've blown it, he thought, and he lit it again. A minute later he returned with the chair, and the candle was out again. No problem – he rekindled it, and this time closed the front door tightly. Then he positioned the chair in the back of the main room to face the front door, and prepared to nap. But just as he began to close his eyes, it appeared the candle snuffed out as if by unseen fingers.

"Hmmph," he said, trying to decide whether he was dreaming.

Just as he was becoming convinced he was indeed awake, the candle flamed up by itself. But before he could deeply ponder this strangeness, Frealaf burst in the front door soaked with sweat, blowing the candle out for good.

"What's wrong?" said Anlaf, but his son could offer no coherent explanation. "Candles lighting themselves, the boy running around like a frightened puppy . . . what next?" thought Anlaf.

That evening they put Frealaf to bed early, and Gudlaug went outside to fetch the other chairs she had left out in the sun while Forthred caught up on his nap on the chair that was already inside. Gudlaug came running in the house saying she had seen a little man run out of and back into the garden.

"Thieves, eh" said Anlaf.

He picked up his axe and went outside to look for trespassers. But after a diligent search, he could find no footprints, no evidence of any men, little or otherwise.

"What did he look like?" said Anlaf as he walked back in the door.

"Little. Bout half as tall as Frealaf, brown leather coat . . . and ugly. Had these weird eyes. I saw them when he looked at me; that's when I came back in," said Gudlaug.

"Well, I couldn't find hide nor hair of him," said Anlaf. "We'll lock the door real tight tonight. And check the windows!"

Anlaf then brought in one of the barn dogs to sleep by the front door. Gudlaug usually insisted that these dogs stay outside, but tonight she did not object. When Anlaf finally turned in, he put his axe close by his bed.

"Strange things happening lately," he thought before sleeping. "Maybe everything will be back to normal tomorrow."

Unfortunately, Anlaf's hopes were not to be realized. In the days to come, things would get much stranger; yes, much stranger indeed.

Chapter 7
Beautiful Morning, Dark Night

The same day that the two boys had set out for the pond, Queen Erinndis went out for a morning walk. Rising on painful knees, she needed to loosen up by doing some mild exercise. She took breakfast up in her room. After that she left with the guards at her side. Soon they approached the great wooden gate of the castle. Strong men swung the creaking gate open, and the troop took off toward her gardens.

They walked down a well prepared dirt path through the gardens. The white and pink flowering trees of the Orchard grew larger as they drew closer. Some of the trees in this orchard were ages old, having been a part of the great mountain forest before farming separated them from the mountains many long years ago. Some said that the roots of the trees fed on an undiscovered bed of emeralds. The mystical powers of the Orchard were equaled only by those of the mountains that circled the kingdom.

Finally they entered the woods, whereupon the path widened into a walking-road, which was kept smooth by workers hired from among the poor (this was one of the Queen's ways to help her less fortunate citizens). The guards fell back and did not talk, giving her time to contemplate quietly.

Even the guards felt their cares melting away in the midst of these boughs. The white and pink flowers were sprinkled liberally among the bright green leaves on their right and on their left as they nearly glided along the path. The scent of flowers played in the wind, beckoning her further down the path. The melodious songs of hidden birds were carried along by gentle breezes into the ears and heart of Erinndis. Shafts of sunlight broke through now and then to give a golden tinge to the forest green in spots. The gentle caress of the warm sunlight also seemed to lessen her constant chill. Walking down this path was like walking into paradise.

Slowly, the Queen and her guards rounded a right turn in this path. She felt renewed energy on these trips and the pain in her knees nearly vanished. The path wound around somewhat but took a general rightward direction until finally they were all headed back to the castle.

Today the Queen came home from her walk there feeling refreshed. She would need all of her new energy, for the affairs of state would take their toll on her as the day wore on.

At length they came back to the great wooden gate. Strong men opened it and the whole procession returned to the castle. It was now nearly noon . . . time for the Queen to take a light meal and then meet with her counselors, who taught her about everything from dealing with international threats to how to pay for patching holes in the wall around Edlad.

After that, Erinndis spent the rest of the day in quiet meditation and rest, for her pains had slowly returned after the healing effects of the Orchard. She again looked forward to sleep at night.

When night time did arrive, parents tucked their children into bed all over the kingdom. They thought that all was well, just as it had been for some time. This night, however, was to be different; as darkness fell, many cherished beliefs would fall with it.

. . .

The night was warm, dark and moonless. When the midnight hour had arrived, the wind ceased its soft sighing, the leaves in the forest hung still, and the air chilled. Then trembled the stars of remotest space, for something had disturbed the peace of their rest. Something invisible to the eye, except for the occasional wink of a distant star passed by an unseen wing.

High above the highest mountain, something rode upon the loftiest of the silent winds. Something that called the howling darkness its dwelling place had awakened, and was even now gliding toward the beautiful city.

For I tell you that there are things that might touch a wall, but they cannot pass through it. And there are things that might not touch the wall, and yet . . . those are the things that come in the night to trouble the dreams of men. And it is from those things that we pray God to guard us till morning's light.

We pray for God's shroud . . . I speak not of a shroud to keep the body warm; I speak of that which protects us from the icy touch of things from beyond the wall.

Chapter 8
Alfric's Farm

"Have you been having problems with rats too?" said Anlaf to Forthred, who had come to pick up some elm.

"Sure have," said Forthred.

"I've never seen this many rats. The farmers must be having a really bad time if they've got them too. I wonder what is going on down the valley?" said Anlaf.

"My uncle Cnebba stopped by yesterday. He doesn't hear or see so well anymore, and I am going with him, for the way is dangerous. I'll tell you what. Along the way I'll make sure we stop by some farms and ask about the rats," said Forthred.

The next day, Forthred and Cnebba walked

through the front door of Alfric's farm house.

Alfric was sitting at a table in the center of the room with several friends. But Forthred and Cnebba were both hungry, and their eyes locked on to the half eaten piece of mutton lying on a table in the corner of the room.

"That meat sure doesn't look very good," exclaimed Forthred as he waved away the flies.

"Eh?" said Cnebba.

"Emma will clean it up," said Alfric. "EMMA!" he yelled, but no one came.

"Any ale today?" said Forthred hopefully.

"Sorry . . . ran out yesterday afternoon," said Alfric . Then, looking back at his friends, "Nasty rats, they're everywhere!"

"Yeah, something's been wrong ever since right before first moon. The wife says, something evil blowing in the wind at night. The rats started getting bad right about first quarter moon," said Cenfus.

"And I've never seen so many and so large," said another who sat at the table. "You wouldn't have any extra cats I could take with me?" he continued.

"Sorry, I've not enough cats to keep them out of my own house," said Alfric. "And they're fighters! I've never seen such big black rats more willing to stand up and fight cat, dog or man. I've had several dogs sicken and die after a scrap with a black rat."

"I hear tell that if you put pieces of sponge in the water, the rats that drink it will swell up and die," said Cenfus, another visiting farmer.

"Nonsense," said Eadward, raising an eyebrow. "You want to mix the root of hellebore with some honey and wheat flour, and leave that out for them."

Forthred did not know how to make things like this, but he wanted to chase them from his lumberyard, so he decided he would ask Gudlaug, Anlaf's wife, if she thought this mixture was a good idea. He pulled out his own skin of ale, for ale, he thought, would help him remember the formula Eadward had mentioned.

"Lots of rats around lately . . ." shouted Cnebba, chewing on the spoiled mutton.

"I heard that the sorceress beneath the mountain said . . ." began Cenfus.

". . . and furthermore, even my cats are fraid of em," finished Cnebba with a fist on the table, before stuffing another bite into his mouth.

"What did she say?" said Eadward to Cenfus in a hushed voice.

"What did who say?" said Cenfus.

"You know, the woman," said Eadward.

Eadward seemed reluctant to say the word 'sorceress.' Perhaps that was because he was afraid that saying the word would somehow reveal his interest in sorcery – an interest of which he was ashamed.

"Oh, her," said Cenfus, gathering his thoughts. "She said that the rats were coming up from holes in the mountain caves. Coming right under the Great Mountains . . ."

"Pshaphatsh!" interrupted Cnebba, spewing meat from his mouth. "There's maggots in this mutton!"

"How long you been eating on that meat?" laughed Forthred.

"Quiet!" said Eadward.

"Fight?" yelled Cnebba, eyeing the door. With meat and saliva running down his white beard, he knocked over his chair as he rushed out to see it. All those seated around the table erupted in laughter.

Eadward took Cenfus by the arm and pulled him toward one of the bedrooms so they could talk.

"What else did she say?" he asked, the gleam in his eye revealing intense interest.

"Well, she said. . . I mean, someone told me that she said . . . that her friends on the other side of the mountains were fixin to come back into the kingdom. Said they had some kind of magic stronger than . . ."

"Than what?" said Eadward, who now feigned no disinterest.

". . . stronger than the Emerald," whispered Cenfus.

Sweat appeared on Eadward's brow as a wave of anticipation swept through his chest. He had always harbored an interest in magic, sorcery, and anything bizarre or strange, and now it looked like maybe his desire to be near such things could be soon realized. And magic stronger than the Emerald? That took his breath away. But he said nothing, for things like sorcery were against the law in Kara Mundalyn, and he did not want to risk appearing too interested in them while they were still illegal.

Eadward ran back in to the front room and gathered up his things with haste so he could ride immediately back toward Edlad and share this gossip with his wife, who shared his interest in things uncanny. But just as he was walking out the door, an irate Cnebba blocked his path.

"Couldn't find no fight out there, you lying rat!" he yelled.

Eadward was speechless. Cnebba gave him a kick in the rear end, sending him staggering out the door to his horse.

"What the . . .?" said Alfric. Hordes of black roaches were swarming into the room where the friends were speaking and crawling under the table. The men stomped on some of the roaches but when more kept coming they got up and went out of the house.

Just then, a woman's scream was heard coming from within the house.

Emma, Alfric's visiting cousin, came running

out of the door, flapping her skirt and jumping up and down. She liked roaches even less than the men did, and she wasn't about to stay inside of a house which was being overrun by them.

Forthred surveyed this scene and decided that there was no more information to be gained by staying with Alfric. He swayed slightly as he turned toward his horse, for the skin of ale he brought with him had been a large one.

"Well, I'm off. We haven't had these roaches up in the forest yet, but I'm going to ask Gudlaug how to mix that hellbone wheat and honey flour anyway," said Forthred as he mounted his horse. "Better to have it and not need it than need it and not have it, I always say."

"I'm hungry. Have some good mutton at home. Want to come?" said uncle Cnebba.

And with that they both galloped off toward Cnebba's house.

• • •

The Queen woke with a start. She had been jolted from sleep by a dream of a huge shape moving through the lower parts of the castle. This dream had been quite vivid.

It is said that sometimes if a dream seems real, it signifies something real. She wondered.

Morning was soon coming, but night was still upon the land. Erinndis stumbled out of bed and put on her nightgown. Taking several castle guards with her, she began to walk by torchlight around the castle; now ascending a set of stairs, then descending into hidden rooms.

She was not certain what she was looking for, but she felt quite restless. Despite her great pain, tonight she felt a restless need to move and explore. The castle was a foreboding place when the sun went down, but on this night the darkness seemed even deeper than usual.

Suddenly there was a rumbling, and everyone felt slightly off balance. All reached for the wall to steady themselves, but the wall itself seemed unsteady, and a few pebbles fell out of the cracks in the ceiling. Finally it stopped. The guards stood looking at the Queen for direction. The Queen looked back at them, momentarily without any direction to give. Something had shaken the kingdom of Kara Mundalyn.

Perhaps the earth itself had prophesied that night, for in the coming weeks a new and frightening plague struck the kingdom. People began to die at a terribly high rate. There was no cure and no known defense against it. Dead bodies appeared in doorways every morning, having been laid there by those still alive in the house. In the cities death carts rode the streets, piling bodies on until they could hold no more. Whole villages were soon depopulated, for those left alive fled from areas hit hardest by the plague. In so doing, however, they brought the plague with them wherever they went.

The epidemic swept the countryside, and the cities where people fled to escape it soon became even worse. But the might of the Emerald held the disease in check in Edlad. The forests, also, were relatively free of roaches, rats, and plague . . . maybe that was because people could not flee to those remote areas and so did not bring the plague with them. However, there were some of these pests in the woods, and those who already lived there hunkered down in their homes, locked the doors, and stayed warm by their fires.

Chapter 9
The Darkness Grows

Deep in the night, Odanae was in his bedroom . . . alone . . . listening to barely perceptible noises scraping somewhere outside. As the darkness grew, so did his fear. Why did big brother Frealaf have to be away at Aldhelm's tonight? He pulled the blanket up around his head; he shivered. He thought about the hideous shapes that must surely be outside. Was it wind? He thought not. Animal? He hoped. Something else? He feared.

Maybe the rats had finally arrived in the forest. Maybe it was something worse. Not knowing, not understanding. A thrill tingled through his belly and up his back as he continued to ponder the thought that some unknown may be outside. Why was the familiar room so alien to him tonight? His body tensed as terror gnawed at his gut.

Then he must have slept, for he had a vivid dream of a large shadow with holes where eyes should be gliding through the wall of his room. He woke quickly . . . was it really a dream? He cried out for mother and father. They came with a candle and swung open the door to their boy's room. The candlelight revealed Odanae's eyes locked the wall . . . as if something was there, but Anlaf and Gudlaug could see nothing.

Anlaf was not easily shaken. That must have been some nightmare, thought Anlaf as he looked at the face of his son, but he said nothing, preferring to leave such things to his wife Gudlaug. Gudlaug tried to comfort her son, saying "It was just a bad dream. We're here now."

Odanae's eyes still opened a little wider whenever they flicked back toward the wall, and tonight his fears were not greatly comforted by his mother's words. Anlaf himself began to feel that something was wrong with this night. He had the strange feeling that something was probing his thoughts for weak spots, and that was a feeling he didn't remember ever having before, and a feeling he didn't much like. What could he do for his frightened son?

Anlaf went back to his room, opened a creaky trunk, and got out an old cloak that had been given to him by his own father. Then he returned to his son's room.

"Here," said Anlaf to Odanae. "This cloak was blessed by the priests of Edlad fifty years ago. If fear comes again, wrap yourself in this." He then laid the cloak on the boy's bed.

After Anlaf and Gudlaug had gone back to their own room for good, Odanae slept again. But then his eyes shot open. The room had taken on a strange dreamlike quality. It was much later now, deeper in the night. Odanae realized that he was aware of himself in his bed, but he was not sure whether or not he was dreaming . . .

He peeked out from under the blankets. The darkness of night enveloped the room, and Odanae could barely see a dim outline of the room's largest features. Shadows merged and separated from each other in the darkness that hovered in the corners. At such times it was hard for him to tell where the darkness ended and his own fears began.

The wind, ever rising and falling, moaned around the roof outside, almost like the sound of women wailing.

He pulled the covers back over his head – then he froze. What? The wind had stopped.

What was that? A strange sound, like an unusually lonely moan, seemed to come from behind the wall. Barely audible, yet (the boy thought) definitely there. Then it stopped. He lay absolutely still for a moment; then he thought, did I really hear that?

Again and again weird sounds came from the wall, and when Odanae was almost used to it, it changed; now it was a little like the moan but also a little like a muffled voice. It said:

"Odanae, Odanae . . ."

He neither moved nor breathed.

"Odanae, Odanae, sing softly tonight . . ." said the voice.

Then he heard something in the darkness snarling, sort of like a dog but deeper-throated. Yet this sound faded in and out . . . was it really there? Odanae felt his will weaken; he had nothing left to with which to fight; the fear in his room had penetrated all his defenses. Fear washed over him like a bath of fire; little faces seemed to be peeking in and out of his wall.

He almost started to sing a strange little song that had come into his head, but was jolted out of it when a huge hooded shadow rose at the foot of his bed. This was no dream; he was wide awake. He tried to cry out, but his voice failed him. The shadow leaned farther, coming slowly; beneath the hood there were holes where a mouth and eyes should be.

With one last, great effort, he reached for the cloak his father had given him and pulled it over himself. The moment the cloak was over him he felt he had put at least some barrier between himself and whatever was in the room with him. Still, something very strange was swirling around him in the darkness. Trying to get at him. Probing at the cloak. Odanae wrapped himself in it as tightly as he could and held on for dear life.

Anlaf wakened suddenly when he heard eerie sounds coming out of his son's room. Without thinking, he leapt out of bed, rushed to Odanae's door, and flung it open. In the twilight he encountered something he would never forget.

His son's room seemed to be filled with the whispering voices of men and women.

"Who's there?" Anlaf yelled.

The voices fell silent. For a second, all was still. Then, a deep voice neither animal nor human seemed to fill the house --

"Obey the Dethtrogh."

Even the fearless Anlaf staggered back at the power in that voice. But his son was in there, so he stepped forward again.

"ODANAE!" he roared in the doorway.

At that, all the chaos in the room ceased, and Gudlaug came running to find out what the noise was about. Odanae poked his head out from underneath the cloak; his wide eyes spoke of unspeakable fear. Later on Odanae could not clearly remember the events of that night. The only thing he did remember was the most horrible dream he had ever had.

Chapter 10
Second Trip to Edlad

"Terror stalks the land. Dare we attempt such a journey?" said Gudlaug.

"How else can we reach the City of Refuge? There is no way to get there except through the countryside," replied Anlaf. "Odanae is so sick. No one around here can help him. Only by leaving the safety of the forest can we reach the Emerald of Edlad."

This is the way the country folk referred to the Emerald of Healing, the greatest of all the healing gems. All gems glitter in the sunlight, but the healing jewels glow with their own light after the sun has gone to bed. No rain can quench their candles; no storm can blow out their lights: for the flames burn wholly within the gems themselves. When the sick are brought forth, that inner fire grows, and when the light touches one in whom flows innocent blood, he is healed.

Poor Odanae had been quite ill since that horrible night. Most of the time he refused to eat, and was now thinner and paler than he was before. Since that night, it hurt him to look at sunlight, so they had to wrap him in a cloak made of sackcloth to travel outdoors. But thankfully he was not sick with the plague that devastated the surrounding countryside.

"Let us not stop and visit with anyone. Let us go swiftly and privately, having no contact with anyone who might have the plague," said Gudlaug.

"Forthred and Aldhelm are going too. They are already waiting for us. We will pass by that way and leave together," said Anlaf.

And so it was that Anlaf and Forthred and all who were theirs began the journey to Edlad, hoping to talk with the holy men and obtain a cure for Odanae. With a crack of the whip, the lumber wagon began rolling along the thick forest trails.

Unlike the previous trip, the weather seemed to have turned somewhat nasty, and wind and pelting rain made this trip most uncomfortable. Fortunately it was summer time, so the cold was not too severe. But no one has ever enjoyed pulling a wagon wheel out of the mud, which Anlaf and Forthred had to do more than once on this trip.

The nights were dark and the days were usually not much better, for winds blew and clouds covered the sun. As Gudlaug had advised, they scrupulously avoided contact with people.

It turned out to be easy to do, for no one was interested in making contact: all who were not sick tried to meet as few strangers as possible, and most of those who were sick never left the spot where they fell.

Whenever the odor of disease and death entered the nostrils of the party, they turned and went another way. The trip ended up taking quite a bit longer than the three days it took in good times.

One night, the party sought refuge in a forest half way between the great forest from which they came and Edlad to which they were going. On this night sky was clear, and the moon was full. The caravan made camp in an area beneath a rocky outcropping protected on the open side by tall trees. Immediately beyond these trees was a ridge from which they could look down and see a forest road, ghostly white in the moonlight. They lit no fire, hoping to remain invisible.

Later that night, Aldhelm heard some sounds not too far off. He looked out from under his blanket. In the trees at the edge of the camp, something seemed to be snuffling around. Or several things . . . Aldhelm could not be sure. He had keen night vision, and he strained to see what might be in the bushes beneath the trees. From the direction of the noise, he thought he could make out several dimly glowing spots, maybe eyes, peeping in and out of the darkness.

What kind of animals could these be? He had lived in the forest and never seen anything just like them, but then again he knew the night could play tricks on your senses, and mundane objects can take on weird and fantastic appearances in the darkness. Aldhelm heard Odanae groan painfully in his sleep. Suddenly, the spots and the noises vanished.

A minute or so passed, and Aldhelm was wide awake and attentive. The snuffling noise did not return, but now he thought heard a different sound, further off, coming from the direction of the road below. He crawled out of his blankets and up to the trees to look down. Below, a mighty army approached -- dreadful warriors, shields and spears glinting in the pale moonlight. No one was speaking on this night march; only an occasional clink of metal was heard along with the padding feet.

Aldhelm was filled with wonder at this sight and leaned forward to get a better view. He put his hand on a branch to pull it out of the way, but it broke with a snap. Some of the marchers below seemed to react to this noise, slowing their march. Aldhelm held his breath and did not move. Then the marching resumed, and Aldhelm relaxed a little. Still, he did not move.

As the last marchers were disappearing in the distance, Aldhelm quietly backed himself up and crawled back to camp.

"Where have you been?" whispered an annoyed Forthred.

"I . . . I have been to the edge, and I saw a great army," said Aldhelm.

"Of course you did, we all heard it passing. Son, you do not know what manner of man may be walking that road. Do not leave without my permission again," said Forthred.

"Yes sir," replied Aldhelm.

Everyone had started to fall back to sleep when suddenly about a dozen men with swords burst out of the woods from all directions. Gudlaug, Aldhelm, and Frealaf huddled around Odanae as Anlaf and Forthred reached for their axes, but it was quickly obvious that they would be no match for their captors, since other soldiers began appearing behind them. The night marchers had heard Aldhelm in the trees and then silently doubled back and crept up on the party.

Anlaf breathed a sigh of relief when he noticed that the shields of the captors were adorned with the lion and crossed swords of Kara Mundalyn. They were in the hands of the army of their own kingdom.

"Who are you?" said the captain sharply.

"I am Anlaf the Lumberjack, and this is my friend Forthred. Behind are our children and my wife," said Anlaf.

"What is your business here?" said the captain.

"We travel to Edlad to seek healing for my son, and grain for my friends here," said Anlaf, motioning toward them.

"Your son is sick?" exclaimed the captain, and the soldiers stood back.

"Not with the plague! Not with the plague!" said Anlaf.

The warriors relaxed a little.

"He has been afflicted, but not with the scourge that now fells so many of our countrymen. You may look at him if you wish. Do you think that my friends would travel with us, if my son had the plague?" said Anlaf.

"No, they wouldn't," said the captain. "You are obviously from Kara Mundalyn. I am sorry for speaking harshly but there is much danger in the land. It is not just the plague . . . our kingdom is under attack. We march to relieve our Eastern defenses. Though the Great Mountains still guard us, the castles on the border are under great pressure from the men of Snagov and maybe other attackers. Many others are now headed to Edlad seeking safety. Yet I fear that even in Edlad safety may soon be a thing of the past."

"How could this be? For they cannot get through the mountains," said Forthred.

"Nevertheless, they attack. Our orders are to throw them back, and that we will do," said the captain. "We must make haste. May you have a safe journey to Edlad."

And with that, the warriors vanished into the night. After about a half an hour of talking, the party settled down to sleep again.

At dawn Anlaf and Forthred arose.

"Get up, get up," said Forthred to Aldhelm. "Time to break camp."

They had barely gotten everything packed when there was a tumult on the road below them; not the quiet marching of troops that had been last night, but the noisy thundering of horses approaching with great speed.

"Get back," yelled Anlaf and Forthred to the boys as they pulled out their axes and ran to the overlook.

It was not long before a large company of knights rode up. There must have been hundreds of them – maybe thousands. The knights saw but took little notice of the party, maybe because it was not dark and it was obvious from looking that this was a little band of people who were not foreign.

The knights chose this spot to dismount and water their horses, as if preparing for further riding. Anlaf found out by asking one of the knights that their leader was Heorogar, a great and powerful Knight indeed.

After about an hour the same company of troops that had investigated the camp the night before came marching quick time down the road. It appeared that they had turned back from their former mission and were hurrying to meet the knights.

"All able bodied men report to me," said Heorogar in a powerful voice. "The enemy has somehow crossed the mountains, we know not how. We must now rally in this spot to meet them and crush them. You . . ." Heorogar said, glancing at Anlaf and Forthred,

"Can you bear weapons?"

Anlaf and Forthred pulled out their axes.

"You may join us if you wish," said Heorogar.

"Yes, but my wife and children . . ." began Anlaf.

Heorogar glanced over at the women and children. "No one is safe anywhere now. If you can put your families in that wagon over there and follow along with us, you will be safer than you would be anywhere else. If we are successful we will escort you to Edlad, where you may find refuge."

There was no time for further discussion. Anlaf and Forthred decided to follow along with the army. Those foot soldiers who could not ride began to build fortifications on the high ground where the party had made camp the night before, and Anlaf began throwing anything he did not need off of the wagon to make it lighter for a quick ride. The knights prepared themselves in the forest and when they appeared ready to go, Anlaf pulled up the wagon behind them.

And so they rode out to battle that day in the shining sun under a cloudless sky, passing through the gentle sloping hills with their villages and farms, and then coming again to a more wooded area. As the sun rose towards its apex, they came out on to a grassy plain, a field, on the other side of which was a ridge of low hills. It was just then that the scouts reported that an army of Gthonic knights were massed on the other side of the ridge, with another army of unknown origin close behind them.

As the sun rested at its greatest height, ready to begin rolling slowly down toward the West, the battle commenced with a blood curdling cry and a furious Gthonic charge. As they approached, the captains of the archers waited, and then at the right moment cried "loose!" and the archers began to release volleys of arrows that felled some of the enemy knights. They were well timed volleys, for the captains were experienced archers themselves and had the best eyes, to judge the right distance and time for the release of arrows.

But the Gthonic charge continued unabated, for when one fell another took his place, and their numbers seemed endless. The knights of Kara Mundalyn roared out to meet them and they met in a tremendous clash. Some were felled by arrows, and some by the sword; and some were felled by the great spears that the knights carried in their charges. Heorogar and his knights fought with terrible ferocity, for he had drilled them endlessly to do just that.

The two lumberjacks and their families pulled the wagon behind the friendly troops as strategically as Anlaf could manage, but the tumult of the battle sometimes caught up with them.

"There! Behind you!" yelled Forthred to Anlaf, and sure enough, riding up on the wagon were four horses, three of them carrying Gthonic knights and one carrying some creature in a brown cloak that looked uglier and uglier the closer it got. Two of the knights drew swords as they approached and one of them pulled out a long spear, which he pointed at the wagon. The four riders pulled up and stopped less than a hundred yards from the wagon. They seemed to be laughing amongst themselves.

Then the knight with the spear suddenly spurred his horse and charged at the wagon. Apparently, they thought to make sport of the unarmed travelers. They had not reckoned with the lumberjacks. Forthred pulled out his axe, leapt off of the wagon, and with expert timing he splintered the spear of the charging knight and knocked him off of his horse. The knight went scrambling off on foot in one direction while the horse ran in the other direction.

The knights with swords then rode rapidly up, and the fourth horse rode up slowly. Anlaf grabbed his axe to join Forthred in the defense of the wagon, as Aldhelm in the wagon readied his bow. But the men of Snagov saw the approach of some of Heorogar's men from afar, so they turned back and rode off with great speed.

The strange creature on the fourth horse, however, just sat and leered at them; not close enough for them to quite make out its features, but close enough for them to discern its extreme ugliness, with a head that resembled a rotten melon and a pair of bulging eyes which expressed some strange emotion Anlaf could not interpret. The creature made some sort of gurgling sound, then it too rode off. Looking at this creature produced an uneasy feeling in Anlaf, and he was glad the sun was up.

Aldhelm, looking on from inside the wagon, felt the hairs on his neck tingle. He was sure that he had seen eyes like that before. Last night.

The battle raged for the entire afternoon and into the evening, but in the end, the men of Snagov faltered before the discipline of Heorogar's knights, though they did inflict many casualties upon them. The battle cost Heorogar 500 of his knights and several hundred archers, and many of those who were left alive were wounded.

The men from Snagov were driven off and defeated, but somehow they had come beyond the mountains. No longer was Kara Mundalyn an island of warmth and safety in the midst of a cold, hard world. The world had come into the kingdom.

The remaining knights, victorious but exhausted, provided safe passage for Anlaf and Forthred, for Gudlaug, Aldhelm and Frealaf, and they rode together back toward Edlad, passing many dead bodies of those who had died by the sword and others who had died of the plague. Some parts of the land seemed untouched by troubles, but many parts of the land seemed to have been laid waste. Finally, they were within sight of the stone walls of Edlad.

Chapter 11
Repentance and Healing

A large wooden sign was posted on the great gate of Edlad:

"Fear not: all you sick and hungry may enter in here. All things within our power shall be done to help those in need. Signed, Queen Erinndis."

There were several arrows stuck in the sign, but other than that, the area just outside of the walls seemed to be in much better shape than the devastated land they had just traveled through.

The army rode into the capital and dropped off Anlaf's party at the camp, along with several other refugees that had joined them after the battle. It was a tent city, and many thousands were present. Anlaf was told that the camp containing the plague victims was out of sight, about a mile to the south, but even it was within the walls of Edlad because the sick stopped getting sicker once inside the city. Anlaf and Forthred put up their own tent in a little spot under a tree slightly off to one side of the camp.

Creak . . . creak . . . went the wheels on the food wagon as it slowly rolled along. Odanae was still sleeping inside the tent, and in fact he had slept through most of the trip. He was somewhat feverish but he had been drinking plenty of water, which Gudlaug took to be a hopeful sign. It was evening, and everyone partook of some dried meat and bread from the food wagon.

"Great King above," said Anlaf, "I can't get the face of that thing on the horse out of my mind."

Aldhelm, who was kneeling at the side of the tent tending to his bow and arrows, stopped working momentarily when he heard Anlaf's comments, but he said nothing.

"It was ugly, all right," said Forthred.

"And what was it? I saw lots of animals around where we live, but I never saw anything like that."

"Well I've not seen anything like it either, but I've seen the look it had in its eyes before," said Forthred.

"Oh yeah? What was it then?" said Anlaf.

"Hunger," said Forthred.

Gudlaug wakened Odanae long enough to get him to drink some water, but he would not take any food. Odanae's eyes squinted when the setting sun leaked through the tent's flaps. He pulled the blanket back over his head to shield his eyes, and within a minute he was back asleep. After the rest of the party had finished eating, they settled in to their blankets for the night.

"Greetings, welcome to Edlad," said a kind voice at the entrance to the tent.

"Well, hello there, stranger," said Forthred. "How may we help you?"

Forthred was rarely very open with strangers until he got to know them, but the genuine friendliness and confident tone of the voice at the door had disarmed him.

"My name is Adrastos, the high priest, and I am here to help *you*," said the priest.

"My son is very sick. After that night . . ." said Anlaf, searching for words. "Something that happened in our house back up in the forest, and he hasn't been the same since. Can't stand sunlight. Sleeps all the time. And . . . the thing that happened in our house, in his room, I've never seen nor heard anything like it."

"There was a voice . . ." Gudlaug interrupted.

". . . there was something in his room, I couldn't tell what . . ." said Anlaf.

Anlaf and Gudlaug were talking at the same time, and their story was somewhat confused, and for good reason: neither was sure what had happened.

"Let me see him," said Adrastos. "First let's see if we can ease his distress, and then I will try to help you figure out what happened in your house."

Adrastos went to the back of the tent, where Odanae was asleep. Gudlaug pulled the blanket back to expose Odanae's head. Adrastos laid his hand on the boy's forehead and checked his breathing.

After examining Odanae, Adrastos told everyone to stand back.

"This boy is very sick, but I think we can help him tonight," said the priest.

Eyes widened when he reached into his cloak and pulled out a small sapphire, which glowed with a little blue flame at its center. It was one of the lesser healing gems, and the priest had been using it throughout the night as he walked among the multitudes. For some reason, its flame burned a little unsteadily, as if touched by a gentle breeze inside the gem. It wasn't working quite as well as it once did, yet many were still being helped by it.

Adrastos held the sapphire directly in front of Odanae. As if in response to the sickness, the gem glowed brightly for a minute, and Odanae began groaning and turning under his blanket. But he soon rose and pulled the blanket off of himself. The sapphire dimmed and Adrastos returned it to its location under his cloak.

Although the tent was now only lit by candlelight, it was obvious to Frealaf that his brother was feeling very much better, for he was no longer sleepy and his eyes were bright. Tomorrow would be the real test, to see how he reacted in the sunlight, but Odanae looked so well already that no one doubted he would be okay.

Adrastos took Odanae outside the tent to talk to him about the events of the night he became ill. The sapphire had so strengthened the boy that he was willing to talk about it freely, although when the interview was over Odanae seemed exhausted. Adrastos instructed that Odanae be put to bed for the night and allowed to sleep late in the morning.

"I'll be back tomorrow night to check on your son," the priest said to Anlaf. "It is very important that you not move your tent until I can see you again. Do you agree to wait for me?"

"Of course. You have helped us so much, and I am very grateful. Any time you need something from me, just ask," said Anlaf.

It was unusual for Adrastos to make a return trip to see anyone twice, for many needed his help. But this was an exceptional case.

• • •

The next day as Gudlaug was preparing lunch, a familiar figure came walking by the tent.

"Hey," yelled Forthred at his uncle Cnebba. "What are you doing in these parts? I thought you had enough food to last you at least a year."

"What've I got to fear, you say? Well I've got to wear this cloak, or the guards might see me.

Overdue taxes, you know. But I wanted to come down to see what I could do to help," said Cnebba.

"Never thought I'd hear that coming from you," said Forthred.

"What am I going to do?" Said Cnebba. "Well, some women gave me this little pouch here, and I'm supposed to go around and ask the mothers if their babies won't eat. If they won't I'm supposed to have em rub some of this stuff on their lips. They say it'll make em suck."

"Where's the dog?" said Aldhelm.

"Eh?" said Cnebba.

"WHERE'S THE DOG?" yelled Forthred and Aldhelm together.

"Oh, him. He disappeared about the time I got to Edlad. Have no idea where he's got off to."

Gudlaug brought out lunch and they all ate.

"Well, guess I'll head out and look for more babies," said Cnebba. As he walked away he continued talking to no one in particular.

"Old and useless, I guess. Brought my axe all the way from home . . . they say they don't need it. Got me nursing babies . . "

Cnebba continued muttering to himself as he disappeared over a small hill.

"He does love to use that axe. Tree cutting champion back in his day. I guess he won't get to show off that swing of his," said Forthred.

. . .

"You boys be sure to come back before it gets dark," said Gudlaug.

"Sure. They said we could have all the water we can carry at the spring," yelled Aldhelm as they carried the empty skins over the hill.

About halfway through the camp, Frealaf noticed that he had taken the skin with a hole in it. Aldhelm decided to continue on while Frealaf ran back to get the good skin.

"Umph!" someone tackled Frealaf from behind as he ran, and shoved his face into the dirt.

As Frealaf struggled to raise his head out of the dirt, he felt an arm tighten around his neck. Someone was lying on top of him and cutting off his air.

"I'm going to put you to sleep," said a voice.

It was Eadgils.

It was just such a moment as this that Frealaf had been preparing for by practicing with Aldhelm. He pulled Eadgils' arm just enough so that he could put his chin under it and take the pressure off of his neck. Now that he could breathe, he used the strength he had gained through constant exercise and the skill he had obtained by listening to Forthred's tips to reverse the hold and put Eadgils in a helpless position. Then he reached for some rope he had hanging on his belt.

"You'd better get ready, because now I'm going to take you back to my father for judgment," said Frealaf as he tied the last knot.

This time Eadgils was thoroughly beaten both in body and in spirit, and he offered no resistance.

Anlaf was at once pleased that Frealaf was now able to so easily defeat his nemesis and perplexed at Eadgils' motives for continuing to attack him. Eadgils fell silent when questioned about this, and nothing short of torture would have made him talk. Anlaf decided not to push it that far but he did threaten Eadgils with dire consequences if he ever tried to hurt his son again. Eadgils swore that he would never again harass Frealaf.

What none of them knew was that Eadgils' father Eadwacer had been experimenting on his son with a talisman of power. Eadgils had felt invincible with his talisman until Frealaf had beaten him in the fight at the pub. This and several other incidents had convinced Eadwacer that his dabbling in things like victory charms might be a mistake, but Eadgils was slower to give up his new obsession and had stolen another of his father's talismans.

When he saw Frealaf walking through the camp alone, he decided to use his new charm to hex Frealaf and give himself mastery over him. This try had been an even more decisive failure than his last try, and now even Eadgils had lost faith in the magic charms. But he would tell no one, out of fear that his father would find out about the stolen talisman.

As it turned out Eadwacer had already found out, but instead of being enraged he was now convinced that the talismans were evil and he was looking through the camp for his son. He knew he had been responsible for Eadgils' exposure to the talismans in the first place, and now he wished to make amends to all he had hurt, especially his son.

After a good deal of back and forth conversation, Anlaf was able to locate Eadwacer and hand his son over to him.

"I know I have done you great wrong, sir," said Eadwacer to Anlaf. "Here are the silvers I cheated you out of. And when you see your brother Forthred, tell him that I forgive his debt, and that I will find him and seek his forgiveness."

Anlaf was somewhat surprised that Eadwacer, who dwelt on a higher level of society than he, would call him sir, but he sensed that Eadwacer was not trying to fool him this time and he took the words to be a real attempt by the moneylender to show respect.

"I never thought I would hear those words from you," said Anlaf. "I accept your apology."

Chapter 12
The Midnight Dance

The sick kept on pouring in to the city. Soon their numbers had become so great that new tents had to be sewn for them. It was at that time the priests Adrastos and Skaldar brought out the Emerald of Healing to them. But when they drew back the red velvet covering, the flame within the Emerald was no longer steady and bright. Instead it was bent over and flickering wildly like a candle on a windy day.

Adrastos stared at the Emerald in stunned amazement.

"No earthly wind can touch that fire," he thought. "Why then does it wane so?"

Suddenly the light within the Emerald dimmed even more and nearly flickered out.

"Behold," whispered one sick man to another, "the fire in the Emerald blows *away* from the priests."

Adrastos instinctively pulled the cover back over the Emerald, as if this could preserve its flame. Then the priests returned the Emerald to its room. No one was healed that night.

Later, the Queen approached Adrastos.

"I want to use the Emerald yet once more," she said.

"Are you sure?" said Adrastos. "Remember how hard it was on you last time."

"I am sure," she replied.

Adrastos paused as if searching for words.

"I am sorry, but the Emerald's powers seem to be at low ebb. Some invisible wind that does not respect the boundaries of stone or gem is trying to snuff its light. I am not sure what would happen if you tried to use it again."

"Please, please, just once more," said Erinndis, tears welling in her eyes.

"I cannot recommend it," said Adrastos.

"Could we not just look at it? Maybe its powers have recovered," said the Queen.

Compassion filled Adrastos' heart, so he granted permission. They walked up the stairs to the high room where the Emerald rested.

"Stand back," said Adrastos, "I do not wish to take the risk we might weaken it."

Carefully he pulled back the velvet cover just a bit. To his surprise, the Emerald's flame was quite bright. Not as bright as it had been in times past, and not as steady, but it was certainly much stronger than it was the night before.

Adrastos bade the Queen approach. As she got nearer, the flame grew even brighter and stronger . . . almost as pure and steady as it had been in former days.

As she bathed in the sacred fire, the youth and beauty of Queen Erinndis returned to her, if only for one night.

Erinndis walked out the door while Adrastos covered up the Emerald and prepared to retire to his room. He knew that when dawn came the Queen would painfully return to her diseased state, at least if things happened the way they did the first time she used the Emerald. There was nothing more he could do tonight, and he needed to rest so that tomorrow he could go out and attempt to minister to the sick again.

After everyone was asleep that night, Aldhelm crept out of his blankets and began to walk back toward where the castle could be seen. How he loved that building! Its beauty was evident even at night, although it had taken on a somewhat more foreboding look in the darkness. A waning moon and the stars were out tonight, and the air was cool and crisp. Aldhelm filled his lungs and walked right out of the camp toward the castle.

The great castle rose majestically into the night sky. Aldhelm had great night vision, and could see the faint glimmer of moonlight coming off of the castle's stones, even though the moon was not full.

As he approached the castle, he came to a stone wall connected to it that went south as far as the eye could see. A little way down the wall was a sort of colonnade of about eight arches. Aldhelm quietly walked up to it and found that he could go right through to what appeared in the darkness to be a wooded area on the other side. There were no castle guards present, so he walked under the arches to have a look.

Immediately he felt his spirit soar. His heart was lifted by the wind's breath that sifted through the pines. These trees were unlike the wilder forest to which he was used, and there was no sense of danger here. Instead, a strange magic hung in the boughs of these woods, and the aroma of the summer night was sweeter here than anywhere else Aldhelm had ever been. He did not know it, but he had walked right into the Orchard of the Queen.

As Aldhelm walked into a glade in this forest, he was surprised to see a girl standing there. He drew in his breath. Never had he seen such grace and beauty as now stood before him. Her white linen dress seemed to glow in the moonlight. She looked at him and smiled.

"What's your name?" said the girl.

"I . . . I'm Aldhelm," said the boy, finding it

hard for some reason to string two words together.

"May I ask, I mean . . ." fumbled Aldhelm, face growing red (which was invisible in the darkness). But the girl knew what he was trying to say.

"My name is Erinnd . . . Erin," said the girl.

"Well hello," said Aldhelm, and then there was an awkward silence. For Aldhelm, anyway. Erin was not awkward at all. She began to move lightly around the grass almost as if she was dancing. Aldhelm could see that she was smiling at him. He did not know what to say, but he recognized the dance as the same one he had seen several times in the village.

Erin put out her hand toward Aldhelm. So they danced softly in the moonlight, the young man and the young lady. Once the young lady slipped in the grass, and Aldhelm had steadied her with his right arm. His strength amazed her, and she smiled at him again.

Aldhelm felt a burst of joy when he lifted her, and for a good while afterwards his right arm still felt warm and good.

Then it was over. They parted, then looked back at each other one final time. The girl gave him that smile again, and then she disappeared into the woods.

"You will never see her again," said a voice that surprised Aldhelm. "You would not recognize her if you did."

Aldhelm was shocked. He had been so caught

up in the experience that he had not seen that she had several people with her. They had tarried behind, some distance from the glade, but now that Aldhelm looked he could see they were there . . . squires of some sort, about his own age. He did not know who they were but they were following after the girl.

He walked away sadly, for he had planned to search the camps the next morning to search for her. How could he have been so stupid! A girl dressed in those kinds of clothes was not poor, and she would not be in the camps anyway. Her station in life was obviously far above his, and he could never be with her. She had won his heart in just a few minutes and broken it in even less time. His pace quickened as he decided to depart this place and try to forget it. But the lump in his throat told him he would never forget. Never . . .

"Cluck, cluck" – came the faint, muffled sound. Almost like hens clucking with their heads under their wings. Aldhelm had barely noticed the strange noise, for he was deep in thought.

"Cluck, cluck" – a little louder this time. He was getting closer to the source of the noise. It was coming from the direction of the colonnades he had entered the woods through. Now he slowed down and took notice, and his forest experience kicked in. The sound was coming directly from the central arch through which he had passed a little earlier.

"Cluck, cluck, cluck." Now he could see them. Three birds facing away from him, two on one side of a tree stump and one on the other. They seemed to be talking to one another and preening.

But that tree stump hadn't been there when he came in a little while ago. Aldhelm froze. Was it a person? An animal?

Using his superb night vision, Aldhelm studied the birds more carefully. No hens these. They looked more like vultures, or buzzards.

"Cluck . . ." suddenly the clucking stopped. Aldhelm knew this probably meant that he had been heard. He squinted; if that shape was a guard, he would be in trouble . . .

"Screeeeech!" came the shrill cry of the birds, flapping furiously and flying off in all directions. At the same time the shape in the middle jumped and with blinding speed whirled around and landed on its feet facing Aldhelm. Aldhelm could see that its body was slightly smaller than his. It was hard to see its face in the half light but the strange eyes and melon head gave it away: it was just like the thing on the horse Aldhelm had seen from the wagon.

Moving like lightening, the creature lunged and wrapped its arms around Aldhelm, digging its claws into his back. Its strength shocked Aldhelm . . . he couldn't move as it lifted him off his feet and flung him to the ground, pinning his arms to his side and his back to the ground. Then he felt a blinding pain on his neck . . . the creature was biting him!

Fortunately, it had bitten into his leather jerkin, otherwise the story of Aldhelm would have ended right there in the dirt.

With a surge of desperate strength, Aldhelm wrestled his right arm over just a little bit; he couldn't free it, but he did manage to grasp his knife with his hand. Using his wrist strength (which was very great for his age) he turned the blade upwards and thrust it into the belly of the fiend on top of him.

The thing let out a ghastly shriek and released its grip just a little. Aldhelm sprung free, then leapt to his feet and faced the creature. With his knife he might be able to fight it. There was no question of running; the creature was too fast. But instead of fighting, the creature turned and ran into the night, sputtering and grunting and holding its belly.

Aldhelm's head was spinning, but he knew the way back to camp. He forgot about stealth or castle guards or angry fathers, and he ran back to his tent just as fast as he could.

Chapter 13
A Spark of Hope

The sun had risen about halfway to its noonday height when Adrastos hastily summoned Healfdene and Heorogar to a meeting.

"We have received a scroll purporting to be from our beloved king Athelgar," said the priest. "The messenger was dead when we found him; the morning sun revealed his body lying at the bottom of a ravine. Though it bears the royal seal, it is heavily damaged and we cannot verify that it really is from the king. Much of it is not legible. I will read those parts of it I can make out."

'Athelgar, by the grace of God king of Kara Mundalyn, to the venerable Adrastos servant in the house of the Lord: Greetings.

It was on this day three years ago that I became aware the Gthonic king had opened the Tomb of the Ghoul; how he found it, I know not . . .'

'. . . creatures of darkness that rise through that cursed hole. Therefore we must . . .'
'. . . bones of the Ghoul were dug up and divided . . .'
'. . . through use of the black arts he brought forth children out of its bones. . .'
'. . . dwelt among the tombs feeding on the flesh of the silent dead;'
'. . . secrecy, so not even you were kept informed, because of the betrayal . . .'
'. . . but he became aware of our plans; and . . .'
' . . . our own blood . . .'
' . . . seal the tomb forever. Little by little we fought our way . . .'
' . . . soon behold your face(s?) . . .'

"And that is all I could read. As I said, it had the seal of the king, but if Wictred destroyed Athelgar's army, it is possible he could have captured the seal and used it to forge a letter as from Athelgar to raise false hope within us."

"But wouldn't Wictred have been able to create a forgery that was undamaged?" asked Healfdene.

"Yes," said Adrastos, "but he is very cunning. He may have deduced that Athelgar puts a code in his letters, not just the royal seal, to further verify its authenticity. He may have created the damage himself in order to make the lack of this code plausible.

The undamaged parts of the missive give just enough information to raise hope within us that our king is about to return with his army. He may have calculated that the risk that we would fight harder because of this hope is outweighed by the probability that we might overextend ourselves if we think

100

reinforcements are near," concluded Adrastos.

"So what can we make of this letter?" said Heorogar.

"We can surmise this much: whether it is a forgery or it is genuine, it is quite possible that we are about to be invaded by the Gthonic army in all its horror. We don't know for sure, but some other signs point to this as well."

"Why would Wictred release such information if he wants to surprise us?" said Healfdene.

"He may not have intended that it fall into our hands so soon. The messenger who bore the letter was dead, having fallen down into a ravine. But we don't know whether this was accidental or purposeful. Perhaps he was supposed to deliver the missive after an invasion was already underway, but suffered his accident before that could happen," said Adrastos.

Then he paused, deep in thought. Finally he spoke.

"We can pray that it is authentic," he said. "If so, Athelgar has resealed the Ghoul's tomb and thereby stopped any further reinforcements the Gthonic knights may receive from the underworld, for Athelgar would not have left the spot alive if he had been unable to accomplish this. And surely Wictred would not have left Snagov if he thought there was any chance our king was still alive. If Wictred himself were to ride against us, Athelgar's return would be our only hope."

That night Adrastos returned to the room where

the Emerald was housed, pondering the multiplying mysteries. Why was the Emerald so weak the night before last, and yet so strong last night? Why even in its strength did its flame waver as it had never done in the past? What of the mysterious missive they had found that morning? Was the king really alive and on his way back? He decided to spend the night in the room with the Emerald and pray. He would seek the answers from the Most High King, for his own powers of intellect had so far failed to uncover them.

Adrastos sat quietly in the shadows in the back of the Emerald's room. His eyes adjusted to the darkness, and he could see the shifting green light coming from beneath the Emerald's covering. For many hours he prayed quietly. Slightly after midnight, he noticed the Emerald's light slowly dimming and shifting more rapidly, almost flickering. He shivered and pulled his cloak more tightly around himself.

Then, he heard footsteps.

The door creaked open slowly. It was Skaldar – apparently seeking to retrieve his staff which he had left in the corner of the room. As Skaldar walked by the Emerald, it dimmed and flickered furiously, its fire shrinking away from Skaldar. After Skaldar had left, Adrastos quietly returned to his room to think, and to pray some more. A thought was beginning to take shape in his mind, and he did not very much like it.

. . .

When Aldhelm staggered back into the tent, Forthred was wide awake and waiting for him with a stick. But Aldhelm was obviously hurt already, so

Forthred held off the beating until he could figure out what happened. Aldhelm had escaped his punishment, at least for one night. But the next morning, Aldhelm was much worse, and Forthred became worried.

"Frealaf," said Anlaf. "Quick . . . run and see if you can find that priest."

Frealaf could not find Adrastos at first, and Aldhelm languished for the whole day. That evening, however, Adrastos came quickly when he heard that Aldhelm had been hurt. When he entered the tent, Aldhelm was lying down and groaning on the same blankets that had held Frealaf several days earlier.

"I would have whipped him within an inch of his life, but when he came in it looked like something worked him over already," said Forthred. "At first I thought an animal tore him, but he said it wasn't. I let him sleep the night, but when dawn was near, he cried out that something was burning his right arm, and he has been lying there ever since."

Adrastos walked back to Aldhelm, prayed, anointed him with oil, and then pulled out the same sapphire he had brought before. The blue fire of the sapphire flamed even brighter than it had in Odanae's case. Aldhelm gave a great cry and then went still.

"Let him lie still for a while," said Adrastos.

After about five minutes, Aldhelm awakened, and though he still had the wound, the fever was gone and he was lucid. His right arm still hurt badly, but it was now bearable.

"Come with me," commanded Adrastos.

Aldhelm sheepishly obeyed, for he was quite aware that he had disobeyed his father and there was something about this priest that made him feel even more guilty. But Adrastos was not there to scold him today. He had other things on his mind. He interviewed Aldhelm much the way he had Odanae, questioning him thoroughly about the creature he had encountered the night before. Then Adrastos dismissed him and went back to talk with Forthred and Anlaf.

"I am convinced, based on my talk with Odanae, on what you have both told me, and now this, that what your son encountered last night was a ghoul," said Adrastos.

"The Ghoul?" exclaimed Forthred.

"No, not *the* Ghoul. That one died a long time ago. This thing was much smaller and less powerful, but it was of the same kind. And if there were enough of them . . ."

Adrastos paused.

"Maybe *that* is why the Gthonic army has proven so formidable this time. If they are riding with many ghouls . . ." Adrastos now seemed to be thinking while speaking "though one would have thought that even men from Snagov would not sink that low. On the other hand, their king . . ."

"So that was a ghoul that we saw with the Gthonic knights?" said Anlaf.

"Don't know yet," said Adrastos, "but I now think I know where to find out. For too long, certain doors have been closed. It is time that someone opened them."

Anlaf and Forthred had no idea what he was talking about, but they could see that Adrastos had made up his mind about something, for he strode off with great haste and a look of iron determination.

Chapter 14
Another Visit Below

The wind was picking up as Adrastos walked toward the castle. Some clouds had begun to appear in the sky, and it seemed that bad weather was again approaching.

He strode into the castle. The first order of business was to check on the Queen. She was now quite ill, and had not even been able to take her walk in the Orchard today. But she was not yet in danger of death.

Then he checked on the Emerald. It had not changed. Its fire was still there, but still not as strong as in days gone by.

Then it was time to take the long walk down to the depths of the castle. Down below the ground floor. Down the stairways where he would need a torch.

The torchlight flickered as it had before, but this time it did not seem to relieve the dusky twilight of the staircase. Today the darkness almost had . . . substance. It was resisting his approach. Going down the stairs seemed even harder than going up. Adrastos was developing a throbbing headache, and even his stout heart was pressed on all sides by a nameless fear. Fear of small spaces was one thing that had never troubled him, yet now the narrowing stone walls seemed to be pushing him away from Skaldar's abyss.

Adrastos was nothing if not courageous, and he kept going. Finally he breathed a sigh of relief when the staircase opened out on the little room at the bottom. The door with the lock on it was closed but obviously much used, for there was a noticeable clear path in the dust going right up to and under that door. Steady lamplight oozed from under Skaldar's door. Bats fluttered out when Adrastos opened it.

"Skaldar?" he cried, but the only answer was his own voice echoing off the hard stones. All at once, a shadow began furiously pumping on the wall. The fear returned with a vengeance; Adrastos wanted nothing more than to run right back up the stairs. But he mastered himself and stood firm. Why did his senses seem so distorted tonight? He had a strong will, but it felt like something at least as strong was pushing against it.

Adrastos prayed fervently:

"My God! I am in darkness! Help me, deliver me . . . my strength is gone."

Suddenly Adrastos realized that the pulsating shadow on the wall was an image cast by the lamp of a large spider shaking its web. A very large spider indeed, he thought.

Adrastos found that he had regained the composure he needed to look around the room. The lamp was growing dimmer, but still providing some light. The table on which Adrastos had earlier placed bread now held many curious instruments, a magnifying glass, a large iron bar, bits and pieces of what at first looked like broken glass scattered about, and several cups containing various potions.

Adrastos recognized some of this . . . they were implements of the black arts, forbidden tools used by those who consort with unseen powers that dwell below. But the magnifying glass, the iron bar, and the broken glass made no sense. He pondered on this for a while.

"My God, he's been breaking the jewels of healing," Adrastos suddenly realized.

Adrastos' intuition was correct: Skaldar had been attempting to somehow extract the mystical power within the jewels to use for his own dark purposes. Many jewels were destroyed in the process. How much success Skaldar had was impossible to determine from the remains on the table, but his intent was now clear.

Adrastos knew that he had to examine the scroll, but only Skaldar had the key to the lock on the door of the other room, in which the scroll was kept.

Avoiding the spider, Adrastos picked up the iron bar that lay on the table. He walked out of the room and over to the other door with the iron lock on it. Iron on iron, he thought, and he wedged to pole behind the lock and began to pull with all his might.

...

The sun had not yet risen, but the glowing light of morning was coming from the east. The trees were lit from beneath with the dawn's orange fire, and a King bathed in its glow just as had the Heroes of the North at the beginning of time, when they stood in awe of the glow that appeared before the first sunrise.

Slowly the King turned toward the now rising sun, and his shield shone with the brightness of it. He and his army had endured years of the greatest torment trapped by hordes of cave giants in the wastelands outside of Snagov, fighting the seemingly inexhaustible reinforcements of strange creatures that kept pouring out of the deep caverns of the earth. But he had vanquished the foe he came to vanquish, the Giant king who ruled on the Black Crag. He had sealed the Tomb of the Ghoul, and now after years of warfare, his army of fearless warriors prepared to return to their kingdom.

Chapter 15
The Emergency Council

Lord Sigeric, Healfdene the Guard, Heorogar the Strong, and Hultirk were still not seated when Adrastos walked in to the Great Hall to convene the emergency meeting. It was late evening, and as twilight rolled in, dark clouds rolled in with it. The priest began the meeting in the usual way.

"I greet you all in the name of the Most High King, whose dwelling is not with men; may He be honored forever," said Adrastos.

"So be it," said all. They were still getting seated when the priest raised his hand to say something, but he was interrupted.

"Why is the Queen not here?" said Heorogar.

"She is not well tonight, and since there is new

information that you need to know quickly, I could not wait for our next scheduled meeting," replied Adrastos.

Adrastos paused and looked at them, then began to speak in a quiet voice.

"As you all know, it has been twenty years since the city of Grod was destroyed in the war. Many of you know that I traveled to Grod right after that. What I am about to tell you now, you do not know," he continued. He took a deep breath before continuing.

"The castle Grod and its chapel were reduced to rubble during the siege. After the fighting was over, I and my colleague Skaldar traveled there, seeking to save what may have remained of the Book of the Traditions of the Fathers and any relics that still survived in the ruins."

The wind began to pick up as Adrastos continued speaking.

"Unfortunately the Book of Traditions housed at that chapel had been burned in the fire, and a very old and valuable copy was lost. When we started packing for the return trip, some debris I was moving fell through a crack in the floor. It was then that we discovered something under the chapel. Its eastern side had caved in to a chamber that lay beneath it. Unknown to us, the chapel had been built on top of a more ancient structure. Its existence had been forgotten until that time.

"Skaldar and I lit torches and descended into the chamber on knotted ropes. As we proceeded to explore it, we found that the room was much more extensive than it looked from above, with openings to stone hallways that went off into the darkness, far beyond what we dared to explore by ourselves.

"For twelve days, Skaldar and I explored what we could of those ruins. There were hieroglyphs of unknown meaning on the walls, and many wonderful and curious carvings of battles and events of which we knew nothing. Fortunately, we were above ground when the whole chapel caved in and resealed the chamber . . ."

As if to punctuate the point, a tremendous crash of thunder shook anything that could move on the stone castle walls. As the thunder rolled off and receded, the wind rose, the torches flickered, and the curtain on the wall began to flap slightly. Adrastos continued.

". . . and so Skaldar and I were not injured. Throughout our explorations of the underground chambers, we found nothing that might explain their existence. We did, however, find a tattered scroll lying on a stone table at the end of one of the hallways. It had the look of great antiquity, and it was sealed with a black seal.

"When we returned to Edlad, we brought the scroll back to our study in the rectory. We then consulted our oldest books of ancient languages. It turned out that the scroll was written in an old variant of one of the Northern languages, similar but not identical to tongue of old Mundalyn."

Again thunder rolled in the distance, somewhat farther away this time. The wind receded slightly, and the curtain on the wall hung in a gloomy silence. The priest then spoke more quietly, and his voice echoed in the hard stone room.

"Much of the scroll contained a history of nations which have long since perished. But at the end of the scroll, there was a chapter that contained what appeared to be spells and incantations . . ."

A wooden door creaked and bumped; the guards immediately jumped up and ran toward it, but then concluded it had been a trick of the wind.

". . . as I was saying, some sort of spells. When I saw these, I said that we should burn the scroll immediately, but Skaldar stayed my hand, saying that much valuable history could be lost forever."

The wind began rising again, and Adrastos had to speak a little louder in order to be properly heard.

"So we decided to preserve the scroll for a time so that its history could be fully translated and re-written, without the spells, on a clean scroll. Only then would we burn the old scroll. Skaldar volunteered to make this translation himself, so I would be free continue visiting the sick and distributing alms to the poor . . ."

All at once there was a crash beneath the table, which caused everyone to jump. Some of the participants crouched under the table, and Healfdene was the first to stand back up, holding a piece of a broken cup.

"It must have fallen off the end," said Healfdene, "Pray continue, Adrastos."

The wind receded again, and again the quiet, intense voice of Adrastos echoed off of the walls.

"The Powers of the Mountains have awakened to fight for goodness, but their influence, so strong in the mountains themselves, does not extend much beyond them. Something has gone over, or under, the mountains and has now appeared in our midst," he said.

Everyone at the table started murmuring among themselves.

"But how in the world could . . ." Lord Sigeric began, giving words to the confusion the rest of the council only felt. His query was answered only by the moan of the lonely wind. Adrastos then began to speak again.

"And now I must speak of matters of central importance, but hard to explain. I refer to the dreams that our children are having throughout the Kingdom. I will tell you of one in particular, a particularly egregious example of what is going on.

"A certain boy named Odanae had dreams in which he was tormented by a being of darkness, which he described to me in detail. He heard its name in the dream. It is called . . . a Dethtrogh."

The mention of that name tightened everyone's throat, though they weren't sure why. Thunder rolled in the distance.

"Odanae had no way of knowing that a such a being is also mentioned in the ancient scroll discovered by Skaldar and myself; in fact, I seriously doubt whether this boy ever heard of such a thing, even in tales older lads tell younger ones around fires at night." Adrastos paused and furrowed his brow.

"What is . . . a . . ." started Healfdene.

"The Dethtrogh is but a shadow-shell emanating from some greater evil," said Adrastos.

"A shadow-shell?" said Lord Sigeric.

"A shadow-shell," said Adrastos, "is the focused energy of an evil power acting at a distance. It is sort of an empty framework -- a form without substance -- that comes forth from some energizing source. As such, the shadow-shell has little power to destroy other than these two things: it has the power to whisper diseases into the bodies of those it visits, and the power to whisper lies into the soul."

"Confound it, how do you know which is real and which is the shadow?" demanded Lord Sigeric.

"No eyes. The Dethtrogh has no eyes," said Adrastos.

At that there was a tremendous crash of thunder, at which even the mightiest of men tensed. The stone walls rumbled and shook. The curtain flapped in the rising wind, and Adrastos had to raise his voice to be heard.

"The real danger is the Evil behind it. As much worse as a Dethtrogh is than an angel, so much worse is the Evil behind the Dethtrogh. And that is the danger I

now realize has come unto us. Skaldar has betrayed us
. . ."

A gasp rose from everyone present at this
horrific news, for Skaldar had access to all the secrets
of the kingdom. Adrastos continued to try and outshout
the wind.

"He translated only the evil spells and ignored
the history. He has consorted with Wictred in secret.
Even now a black image stands in Skaldar's closet, to
which he bowed down. He has summoned the Ancient
Powers that lay dead beneath the earth, which have now
into this very castle . . ."

Huge crashes of thunder interrupted, and a giant
gust of wind blew out all the torches. The meeting lay
in utter darkness, and the thunder shook the walls so
horribly that small pieces of stone clattered to the floor.
The howl of the wind around the parapets moaned like
a chorus of dying souls, and some of the guards cried
out when they saw two faint, whitish balls of light
peeking in and out of the upper windows.

These vanished after a few seconds, but the roll
of thunder did not cease -- instead seeming to drum its
way into the depths of the castle, shaking men's hearts
as well as the stone walls. Without meaning to,
everyone held their breath as the thunder rolled deeper
into the depths of the earth. Finally the ghastly noise
disappeared into the deep; everyone sighed nervously,
and an eerie quiet gripped the darkness of the Great
Hall.

Facing the table, Adrastos lit a torch in front of
his face and then lowered it down; its flame lighting the

curtain on the wall, his giant shadow rising behind like some grim monster.

Adrastos closed his eyes as if deep in thought. Then he bowed his head and prayed silently. Those present knew that the priest could sometimes sense things beyond what other men could see, and this was especially true when he was in communion with the Most High King. At length, he raised his head, opened his eyes, and spoke.

"The Gthonic army is within our borders," he said. "King Wictred is here this time, in consort with the powers of darkness. We are to be attacked from all sides. The living shall attack at the walls of Edlad, and the dead shall reach up from beneath."

Adrastos looked at all who sat at the table with burning eyes.

"Something very evil has been released from beneath the earth; something that each and every one of you will soon have to face," he said.

"There is still a little time, but very little," he said, looking up at the windows above. "We have no time to lose: we have been seen."

With great urgency the men rose from their chairs and hustled out the doors of the Hall. Heorogar knew that he had to get to his knights, Healfdene had to go to his guards, for they would soon be needed. They knew that they could not lose this battle and survive. As the commanders organized their troops on the wall, the thunder continued rumbling in the sky above.

Chapter 16
Into the Darkness

Far away in the land of Snagov, the Gthonic Temple loomed like a black mountain in the last embers of the sunset. The dissonance of warped gongs softly sounded as monks repeated memorized incantations, hoping to commune with the spirits of the underworld. The undisputed master of such communion, Wictred, Lord of Snagov and Gthonic King, slowly walked through the grand entrance of the Temple with seven knights following on foot.

Once inside the Temple the king and his attendants slipped into a side room that was currently devoid of occupants. At the king's command, the knights pulled together the red curtains that served as a door to the room. The knights were elated that they had been chosen to accompany the king. They all had their own ideas at what favor or special assignment the king had in mind for them, but only Wictred knew for sure what dark business brought him to the Temple. Once comfortably inside the room, the king began to speak in a quiet voice.

"Several years ago, we lured king Athelgar out of his kingdom and tricked him into attacking the cave giants of the Black Crag. He foolishly believed he could seal the tomb of the Ghoul, which I opened. At that time I also sent out spirits to give his daughter a fatal disease, so that Kara Mundalyn would eventually be bereft of rulers.

"I also took other steps to weaken the kingdom from within. For years our magic charms and talismans have been flowing into Kara Mundalyn through the rat tunnel under the mountains. After years of preparation, our forces are now within the Mountains of Edlad.

"For too long the denizens of that kingdom have looked down upon Snagov as inferior. For too long Athelgar has horded the gems of healing. What right does he have to them? What use do they put them to? To pray to see who should be healed? No, it is so the priests can decide who lives and who dies. To make the strong stronger? No, they keep the weak and infirm alive against the will of nature. A curse upon them!

"The time to attack is almost upon us. The time has come to conquer that kingdom, and then I shall claim that great Emerald, the so-called Fire of Edlad, as my own."

At this point he rose and began to gesture, as he did in all his speeches.

"That which is, belongs by right to the

strongest; therefore I will take the Emerald as the lion takes the lamb! Nor should the Emerald be named for a place, but for the one strong enough to hold it. It shall henceforth be known as Wictred's Fire!"

The knights felt their hearts leap, for the king had magic in his voice, and this private audience made his words all the more seductive.

The Gthonic king sat down and his tone became more familiar.

"Athelgar still lives. It seems the giants aren't as frisky as they once were," said Wictred with a wink. Wictred could be very charming when he wanted to be. The knights were thrilled because they thought they had been taken into his inner circle. They were wrong. The Gthonic king was merely practicing his persuasive skill to judge its effect on the knights. But they were right about one thing . . . they *had* been chosen for a mission.

"And now I must make the final preparations for the coming war," said the king quietly. "Summon the Priest of Night."

The one of whom the king spoke was he whom no man had ever seen, who had slept in the depths of the earth since the beginning of time, until the dark incantations of Wictred had aroused him.

The hard faces of the Gthonic Knights blanched white at this command, and no one moved.

"Summon the Priest of Night" said the king again.

"Now?" said one of the knights.

Wictred's eyelids began to twitch slightly. Even his powers of persuasion had not been sufficient to create enthusiasm for such a task.

The knights feared the Priest more than death itself, but the immediate danger was the wrath of their king, so they ran from the room, leaving the curtains flapping behind them.

"Don't forget the sacrifice!" whispered one of the knights. And so they grabbed a passing monk and plunged down the dark stairway leading to the subterranean sanctuary where the Priest slept.

. . .

Down and down they went, stumbling occasionally, their iron discipline shaken by the maddening fear of what they were about to attempt.

No spiders down here, for something walked these halls that terrified them as much as they terrify the gossamer lightwings that soar in sunny skies.

Down further and further until all light had faded, and eyes were useless. The knights were not lost, for as part of their training they had to memorize these hallways. They had to be able to locate the door of the Sanctuary of Blood, where the Priest slept, as well as all the other doors in the bowels of the Temple.

But they had never had to *open* the door. Until now.

A cold breeze oozed out from behind the door as it creaked open.

The knights felt rather than saw a deeper darkness in the center of the room. The chief of the knights thrust the monk out in front of him and spoke.

"O thou that dwellest in eternal night, we bow before thee. O thou that dwellest in eternal night, come forth," echoed his voice.

Absolute silence. They waited but nothing stirred in the darkness.

"O thou that dwellest in eternal night, we bow before thee. O thou that dwellest in eternal night, come forth," he said again.

Again, nothing. He began to breathe more easily. Maybe the Priest would not come.

"HAAghgh!" He screamed as no Gthonic knight ever should, for he felt hairy spider like legs embrace not only the monk, but himself as well, with an iron grip.

Then the scream was muffled as if in a blanket, choked silent as the legs pulled both him and the intended sacrifice in toward some invisible arachnid center. The knight had not realized that the monk knew exactly what was going on, and at the last moment had swallowed some strong poison to avoid what was to come. The hairy legs threw the dead body of the monk to the side and pulled the struggling knight in ever closer.

Whether the legs were solid or not, even the victim could not know; they might have been manifestations of projected thought, for the Priest had that kind of power.

Either way the effect was the same. The knight was wrapped in a webby coffin, and whatever was at the center of the legs bit through and sucked his life into itself. The coffin sunk down into the center as the legs wrapped more tightly around it.

Though their eyes were useless, the other knights saw what was happening as if in a vivid nightmare.

Now that the Priest was placated, the rigor mortis that bound the other knights turned to wild panic. They charged out the door and flew up the stairs.

After they left, the legs released the coffin, which immediately began to disintegrate into wispy filaments. What came out of the coffin was so horrible that it had to wrap itself in the life energy of another in order to walk in the land of the living. A life for a life. The life in the blood of the knight now clothed the Priest as It prepared to visit the king. The Priest floated out the door and slowly ascended the staircase.

About an hour later, the curtains to the king's room began to flutter as if disturbed by a gentle breeze. The king rose to his feet as something about eight feet tall split the curtains and stood before him. What stood before the king was not a knight; Wictred didn't know, and didn't care, if any of the knights had survived their encounter with the Priest.

That which stood before the king was the Priest of Night. The king had dealt with the Priest before, but each time was a risk even for him.

"Have you flown over the mountains into Edlad, as you said you would? Have your shadows probed the hearts of the weak? Have they breathed the Miasma of Death into Kara Mundalyn?" said Wictred.

"They have," said a voice from beneath the ground.

There was a long pause. The Priest hovered before the king like an image made of pale moonlight that illuminated nothing but itself. Wictred knew that to rush the Priest could bring swift punishment, which even he could not predict with certainty. With skill obtained during a thousand enchantments, he timed the right moment to speak again.

"Are my armies fully possessed with the powers of darkness which only you can grant?" said the king. "Am I the one to whom they look to crush the kingdom of Athelgar?"

"You are," said the same muffled voice.

Again, there was an unnaturally long period of silence while the king divined the right moment to speak. Again he spoke in the same calm, measured voice that had brought him this far.

"Is the Shadow ready to engulf Kara Mundalyn? Will you stand with me in the battle to come?" asked Wictred.

"I will," was the reply.

"And Athelgar lies dead at the foot of the Black Crag?" the king asked hastily.

This time there was a very, very long pause . . . so long that Wictred, master of sorcery though he was, became concerned and finally had to do some fast thinking.

Wictred resisted the potentially fatal temptation to re-ask the question, and then did something he had never done before any living man . . . he bowed to the Priest. It was the right thing to do. The specter of the Priest started to decompose; and just as an unimaginably ugly face started to become visible from behind the melting cocoon of light, the whole abomination sank through the floor and disappeared.

The king stood for a good moment. He had survived another encounter with the powers of death. He had received almost all the good news he hoped for, being denied certain knowledge only of Athelgar's fate. Full of assurance that he now held the ultimate power, he said to himself: "Tomorrow we ride."

Chapter 17
The Trial of Edlad

The bad weather that had arrived during the meeting in the Great Hall continued unabated for several days, and the ground continued to rumble. On the afternoon of the third day, the dark clouds were so thick that it almost seemed to be night. It was at that time that guards on the tops of the walls heard the thunder of approaching hoof beats.

"Behold, there lies the city of Edlad," cried the advance guard of the Gthonic army. King Wictred the Vengeful opened the slits in his skull that passed for eyes and smiled broadly, revealing two rows of sharp teeth. He was never seen opening his eyelids wide, and no one knew how he could see, for two thin slits of white were all anyone ever saw of his eyes. Wictred was cloaked in a black robe and sat upon a deformed but muscular reddish black horse. Hundreds of Gthonic banners flapped in the rising wind. Armies of tens of thousands of men from Snagov, whipped into a frenzy by the sound of their master's voice, trembled with excitement as they waited for the command of Wictred.

"Now Kara Mundalyn is mine," he snarled. The snarl grew into a laugh, a frightening sound full of the joy of pure hatred. A long bony arm rose out of his black robe, holding his sharp sword high. Then with a quick hacking motion he dropped his sword, signaling the attack.

A horrendous shriek rose up from his men as they charged into the growing twilight. Wind swirled round about, carrying flocks of black vultures who came to pluck the eyes from unsuspecting knights. Thunder rolled both in the dark clouds and under the earth. Flashes of lightening revealed another horror . . . an army of ghouls that Wictred had bred and raised as his own children; multiplying them, holding them in reserve for this moment. These are the children of the Ghoul of old, for Wictred had opened its tomb and, through his black arts, brought pieces of its corpse to life. They feed on blood and flesh as did their father of old, whose spirit continues within them seeking revenge on the offspring of Ealdulf the Bold.

. . .

As the walls of the castle shook and the sounds of battle came through the windows, Skaldar walked quietly up the stairs to the Emerald's room. His heart was lifted up with the thrill of victory, for all was going according to the plan that he had laid out with Wictred in secret.

Now he was at the door. He listened. The sounds outside spoke of death and destruction, but he heard no one inside the room. The guards had all been called forth to the battle and he had the place all to himself. Ever so carefully, Skaldar crept closer to the Emerald.

"Almost done," he thought. "Soon the power shall be mine."

. . .

The whole land rumbled and shook from the thundering under the earth. Blackish purple clouds enshrouded the land between the mountains in a tomblike twilight. Thousands of pairs of glowing embers, which were the eyes of the ghouls, advanced slowly up the hill toward the walls of Edlad, which were even now starting to crumble from the tremors.

Strong knights on the wall doubled over in pain, for the ghouls had the power to send fear and pain to a man's belly with their eyes, and with thousands of them glaring at the wall, even the knights of Edlad were affected.

Wictred's catapults began firing huge boulders flaming with fire over the walls, hoping to divert the defenders from the walls. The catapults continued firing boulders, fire, and yes, even the heads of dead knights, over the wall.

On command, a hail of arrows rained down from kingdom archers who were out of eyesight of the ghouls and so not affected by their wicked gaze. Many ghouls fell, but others kept on coming, and there seemed no end to their numbers.

The efforts of all were needed now as never before. Forthred and Anlaf joined the ranks of the defenders of the walls, raising their axes to hack down those climbing the ladders. The men were no trouble; even with their armor on they were not as strong as the trees these lumbermen were used to felling. But the ghouls . . . even such stout hearts as Anlaf's and Forthred's quivered when they saw those eyes.

Aldhelm had great, great pain in his right arm. Yet he managed to grip his bow and help fire arrows toward the attackers. Frealaf also brought out his bow. The boys discovered that if they avoided the gaze of the closer ghouls and aimed over their heads, they could score plenty of hits. But soon they were low on arrows.

Frealaf was surprised to see Eadgils running up to their position with more arrows for them. Eadgils did not know how to use a bow very well himself, but the fresh ammunition was a very welcome surprise.

"I didn't know you had the guts to come up here," said Frealaf gruffly, although, or perhaps because, his own heart quivered also.

"I'm not afraid," quavered Eadgils.

In fact it was excruciating to Eadgils. His heavy involvement with magical talismans made him particularly vulnerable to the gaze of the ghouls, and his heart shook like a leaf in the wind. But Eadgils had made up his mind that from now on he was going to make friends with people like Frealaf and Aldhelm, and that he was going to prove himself to be a true son of Edlad.

No longer did any citizens of Kara Mundalyn count each other as enemies. They were all in the same boat, and they all knew it.

. . .

Skaldar gently lifted the covering from the Emerald. Its light was nearly out; only an occasional flicker appeared within it, no brighter than the dimmest star that twinkles at the edge of vision. He pulled out a little bag, and raised his hand to grasp at the prize.

But he froze when a deep growl sounded from somewhere in the shadows.

"What the . . .?" he muttered, pulling out his sword and squinting into the darkness.

And out of that darkness bounded a large dog, a dog that knew a thief and a scoundrel when he saw one. Skaldar lifted his sword and prepared to do away with this interruption to his plans.

And so in front of the Emerald there was a battle between man and beast, the man with a sword, the beast with its teeth. When it was over the man was staggering down the stairs without his prize, blood running from his arm as he went. The beast sat contentedly under the Emerald on top of the man's sword, and though it had not eaten, it let out a huge, contented burp.

...

The army of ghouls rolled siege engines up to the wall; by some evil magic these towers seemed immune to the shaking of the earth which was destroying the walls. Soon thousands of ghouls were pouring onto the wall tops like hordes of rats. The defenders left on the walls that could still hold a sword swung and sliced at the ghouls, who hacked back with their axes. The ghouls were incredibly tough and many a knight was felled by their blows.

Warriors slipped in blood and stumbled over bodies in exhaustion, and still the army of ghouls swarmed up the walls.

The Queen looked on from her high tower window, praying as she never had before. She was so sick that she could barely stand, yet she would not let her kingdom go down without doing everything in her power to save it. Right now, all she could do was pray. She looked out upon the carnage with growing horror, and then closed her eyes for fervent prayer.

In the deepest parts of the castle there came a rumbling, a shaking and a groaning of the earth. Something had entered the castle from beneath. A black shadow poured out of the room of Skaldar and shot up the stony staircase. Those few people who were still in the castle to guard the Queen first encountered the shadow on the ground floor, in the Great Hall.

It was a silent darkness that seemed to hush all noise and snuff all lights. A guard standing at the door to the Great Hall was enveloped in this darkness. His sword had no effect on the shadow. It engulfed him; he could not see, and he could not breathe. He fell to the ground dead. And the shadow kept coming.

Another guard stood at the foot of the staircase

that led to the upper floors. Since no blade could fight this foe, he lit a torch. The shadow enveloped the torch and its light became dim. Though the darkness paused briefly to deal with this light, it went out and this guard too fell to the ground dead. And the shadow kept coming.

A third guard stood at the top of the staircase. Seeing what had happened to his fellows, he dropped to his knees and began to pray. "Since no blade or flame can stop this darkness, I will ask the King of Heaven to protect me," he thought. The darkness came up the staircase and enveloped the third guard. As long as he stayed on his knees the darkness could not consume him, but he prayed only for himself and forgotten about the Queen. So although he did not die, the darkness surrounded him and was not stopped. And the shadow kept coming.

But when the darkness was coming close to the upper room where the Queen was praying, it encountered two new things. One was the flickering green light of an Emerald that the powers of death had tried but failed to extinguish. The other was the prayer of a Queen who prayed not for herself, but for her kingdom. Thus was the shadow stalled at the Queen's door; it could go no further at first. But then its icy fingers began to reach through her door.

"No one will hear your whining," a hissing voice seemed to be whispering in Erinndis' ears while she prayed. At that she felt incredibly weak and frightened, but she prayed all the harder.

Suddenly some infernal catapult behind Wictred's lines released what looked like a finger of smoke that reached out and touched the wall of the city; a thunderous crash rang out, and two huge cracks about twenty feet apart appeared in the city wall next to the great gate. The rumbling continued, and after a moment the stones between the cracks fell to the ground. A breach in the wall had been created.

Knights charged in with a shout to block access to the city. They were met by a sea of ghouls who answered with their own horrendous cry. Heads flew off, horses fell, and the battle waxed hot and heavy, the outcome in doubt. At one moment the ghouls seemed to be breaking through, at another moment the knights seemed to be sealing up the breach.

Word arrived that the Gthonic Horde was also entering the city from the gate through which the river passed, and Heorogar put Caelin, his second in command, in charge and rode off in great haste to plug that hole.

Men ran forward in a desperate attempt to construct some sort of wooden barriers to help the knights, but the battle was so fierce that they had little success.

Soon the Gthonic Horde, terrifying in appearance, arrived at the breach. The ghouls made way for them, and the knights Edlad began to fall. The Gthonic Horde began to pour into the city, and the defenders were giving way.

Suddenly, the defenders still on the walls lifted their heads, for an old man with white beard had appeared in the breach, swinging his axe with abandon, slaying ghoul after ghoul. For this man feared nothing.

Even the Gthonic Horde had no answer to his ferocity. His name was Cnebba, a woodsman from the borderlands. His one good eye flashed with anger and he mowed down both ghouls and Gthonic knights with his mighty axe.

Seizing the moment, the knights of Edlad came roaring back into the breach. For many moments it looked like the Gthonic Horde might be pushed out of the break in the wall long enough for defenders to erect some kind of barrier.

It was said that Cnebba fought with the courage of a thousand lions that day. But finally even his mighty arm began to slow, and his axe grew heavy. At length he sunk beneath the waves of ghouls and black horses that now poured through the breach.

The knights gave way once again before the Gthonic Horde. At the tops of the walls, there were now more Gthonic knights than defenders, and ghouls were beginning to feast on the bodies of Edlad's bravest men, sometimes before they were even dead. Their terrified cries pierced any quiet moments hiding between the din of battle.

The Queen could see all things taking place from her high tower, and she struggled not to lose faith or to stop praying, though her throat now tightened from the gathering shadow in her room, and her body shivered violently, for the cold that was always with her was growing worse.

Anlaf, still defending what passed for a front line behind the breach, had suffered a serious wound to his left arm, and was now bleeding heavily. He still swung his axe with his right arm, but the knights he was with were now cut off from the other defenders and trapped against the inside of the wall.

Forthred had joined other knights in chasing a pack of ghouls that had entered the city and descended upon some sick children, seeking to devour them. They had trapped the ghouls and were now cutting them down, but more ghouls were coming in behind them, and Forthred too was trapped. The defenders were putting up their last, desperate fight to keep the invaders from flowing into the rest of Edlad.

It was then that the Gthonic Horde stopped its advance. The only sound now was the munching of the ghouls and the gasps and screams of those on whom they were feeding.

The Gthonic Horde parted in the breach. Through their ranks emerged a hooded figure in a black robe, towering above them on a giant horse.

Flashes of lightening illuminated the figure as it rode slowly through the black knights. When it lowered its hood, all could see that this was none other than Wictred, the Gthonic king. He surveyed the scene, revealing a face that existed nowhere else on earth except in the nightmares of men.

"You are in the presence of the greatest king the world has ever seen or will see," said Wictred in a powerful voice. "I am the hero of the ages, I am the master of time and space. I am he that walked on the fire beneath the earth and did not burn. I am he who has ascended the highest mountain peak and challenged the stars."

When Frealaf heard the sound of that evil voice, he shrunk back behind the wall, his heart beating wildly.

Wictred looked with pleasure at the multitude, knowing that knees now trembled at the awesome sound of his voice.

"Even now your queen is dying from the curse that I put on her when I hurled your king's army into the abyss beneath the Black Crag like so much trash. Now fall down and worship me, and I will allow you to serve me in my kingdom. Why wait any longer?"

He paused again to smile and savor the moment.

"We await the return of Athelgar the Fearless," said a rather unconvincing voice from somewhere on the wall.

"Ha!" Wictred and all the Gthonic Horde laughed hard. "He is not returning. I left him and his army surrounded by cave giants under the Black Crag years ago. Doubtless he has been dead for a long time, slain by the giants or by that which rises from the tomb of the Ghoul, which he was foolishly trying to seal," said Wictred.

"Now why wait? Surely all Edlad shall worship me."

"Not while I live," was the calm voice of a boy. Frealaf rose before Wictred, his bow tightly drawn with a sharp arrow aimed at his head.

Wictred laughed long and hard. He turned on his horse, flashing a rare quizzical look at Frealaf. Then he looked at Frealaf through those horrible slits of white.

"You can look upon me and not tremble?" said Wictred with seemingly genuine surprise.

Frealaf said nothing, but it was obvious that he was not trembling.

"Come back when you have a beard," said Wictred, unable to stifle his laughter.

Frealaf's arrow flew like lightening and struck Wictred in the right eye.

The shriek of the Gthonic king was so horrible that even the ghouls stopped their feeding and cringed. With many terrible curses and blasphemies, Wictred turned his horse and fled the area, the arrow still sticking out of his head.

For a moment the Gthonic Horde was in complete disarray. Ghouls stumbled over one another in confusion, and a great shout went up from the wall, as the defenders of Edlad now began to throw attackers off. Heorogar's knights charged again toward the breach, and hope revived that it might still be possible to plug it up.

But that hope was shaken when the Gthonic Horde came thundering back, order restored. Again they overwhelmed the defense. All hope failed when Wictred came riding back a few moments later. His head was covered with his hood, and it was bowed; but he rode steadily and calmly. Again the Gthonic ranks parted before him.

He rode into the very spot where he had been before. Two Gthonic knights held Frealaf's arms behind him, and a ghoul stood in front of him staring, eyes glowing like two full moons. Anlaf saw that his son was in trouble. He moved into the shadow of the wall and began to make his way toward the breach.

King Wictred slowly raised his head and pulled back his hood. He opened his eyes . . . and to the horror of all, his right eye seemed healed with only a slight scar on the eyelid. A smile again creased the face of the Gthonic king. He dismounted and strode toward Frealaf. Now Frealaf trembled.

"Eat," said the king.

The ghoul sank its teeth into Frealaf as a shout rose up from within the Gthonic ranks, who poured into the breach followed by shrieking ghouls. The remaining defenders began to drop their weapons.

The wind wailed, there was thunder, and all was dark. Then unexpected flashes of lightening caught the Gthonic king by surprise, for both eyes were wide open . . . pure white, no pupils. A long cascade of lightening revealed his head jerking oddly, and he laughed with such a hideous sound that even his own troops shuddered. Then the lightening ceased.

All at once there was a steady glow -- not from lightening -- that began growing in the East. A knight of Edlad standing on a high tower shouted, "The king is coming!"

Then others on the highest parts of the walls – also illuminated from afar – joined in the shout, "The king is coming! The king is coming!"

The Queen's head ached, her knees felt weak, and fear gnawed at her belly, but she never stopped praying, never gave up hope. When at last she opened her eyes, a beautiful white dove, glowing as if illuminated by s shaft of sunlight, flew by her window, peeping softly as it went. She lifted up her eyes in wonder to the mountains in the distance.

The clouds broke a little, and the source of the glow was revealed: a brilliant wall of light shining forth from the East like a thousand tiny suns along a ridge about a mile outside the wall of Edlad. The clouds had broken at high altitude in the West. The light of the sun, still blocked by clouds from those in Edlad, was shining off of the shields of thousands of holy Knights led by their King, Athelgar the Fearless. These had been purified by surviving the bath of blood they endured in battles beneath the Black Crag, far from Kara Mundalyn.

Ghouls stopped in their tracks, frightened by the unexpected intrusion of light, which blinded their eyes and turned their fear back in upon them.

The glory of the sun lit up the whole side of the ridge as the knights thundered down in a furious charge. King Athelgar's gold rimmed blue cloak flapped like flaming fire as he out rode the rest of the knights. Athelgar was the first to crash in to the line of ghouls which was now beginning to form into a defensive position.

Ghoul heads flew off by the hundreds as the clouds broke and the towers of Edlad again gleamed in the sun. The long sought deliverance of Edlad was at hand.

When the knights of Edlad arrived at the breach in the wall, they found Frealaf lying on the ground, injured but quite alive. At his side lay a dead ghoul and a dead Gthonic knight, both of whom had been felled by Anlaf's axe; for he had charged out to save his beloved son. Anlaf himself lay motionless in the dirt in a pool of blood, his right arm nearly severed at the elbow, his hand still tightly gripping the axe.

The defensive lines of ghouls broke in disarray and the Knights of the Kingdom crushed them underfoot. Never again would a ghoul ever be seen in the entire history of Kara Mundalyn, so terrible was that slaughter.

Still, the Gthonic army was strong enough to cause some real problems if only the darkness would return. Wictred still had many ghouls left in his ranks, so he commanded his sorcerers to summon more clouds to blacken the sun, for it was the sun's light that was hindering his creatures of darkness. A few clouds did began to form when they cast their spells, but a mighty wind blowing out of the North scattered them as quickly as they could form. The sunlight was getting brighter, not dimmer – and all evil shadows retreated back into the bowels of the earth, there to wait for some other moment when perhaps they might again crawl out to terrorize the children of men.

. . .

The very shaking of the earth that before had helped the Gthonic army by weakening the walls now fought against them by cutting off their way of escape. A huge crack opened up in the earth right behind what remained of Wictred's army, sending many men from Snagov to death below, and preventing the rest from turning to flee back to lands beyond the Black Crag.

Wictred was now trapped against Mount Hope with just a few of his men and a couple of hundred panicking ghouls. His army began to retreat up the great ledge of the mountain, fighting as they went, but being progressively cut down. Finally, one great charge of the Knights of Kara Mundalyn brought the Gthonic Knights to their knees in surrender, and Wictred was on his own.

"Surrender now. Your battle is over. If you lay down your weapon and shed no more blood, your life will be spared," cried Athelgar.

Wictred would have no part of that. He let out one final blood curdling scream, uttered a blasphemous curse, and then pulled up his horse and charged up the side of the mountain. Heorogar and his knights thundered up the mountain after him.

"There is no way he can escape now," said Athelgar to Healfdene. "The ledge that goes up the mountain is bordered on either side by the greatest chasms known to man, thousands of feet of cliff with a rocky death waiting below for any who falls off. The path goes straight up the mountain to the Face in the Rock, where no man or beast can breathe any more."

When the Gthonic Knights began to retreat,

Queen Erinndis had lifted up her eyes to heaven, given thanks to the Most High King, and then collapsed in exhaustion. Unfortunately she fell forward out of her window on the high tower, her robes fluttering in the breeze as she descended toward earth. But the tree branches had mercy on her and reached over to soften her fall. Squires and citizens knelt around her. She was in bad shape but still breathing, so they summoned the guards. When King Athelgar returned to the city and was told what happened, he quickly rode up to her. For a moment, he was stunned at her appearance, but he did recognize her. He leapt off of his horse and gathered his daughter up in his arms.

"Long have I desired to see you, to have our eyes meet in joyous reunion, and now have you been taken from me?" said he with a catch in his voice. "My daughter, my sweet Erinndis!" he said tenderly as he slowly carried her back into the castle.

After the King entered the door of the castle, the clouds broke even further. Then the light of the Sun reached out and touched the Emerald, streaming through the open window to its room. The Emerald answered back with the most powerful green golden light ever, and for the first time Emerald and Sun shone together. The mingled light of the Emerald and the Sun rained down upon the city of Edlad, liquid light, touching the lips of all the fevered sick and quenching their thirst. Those in the camps that were near unto death were healed, and they stood on their feet and praised the God of heaven.

Anlaf stood upon his feet, healed of his mortal wounds; and he embraced his son Frealaf and took him to find Gudlaug and Odanae. But Aldhelm's right arm, with which he had lifted Erin that night, was still burning with pain. For some reason the otherwise universal healing had not reached Aldhelm.

The rubble in the breach was a chaos of blood, stones, swords, and the fallen bodies of both the good and the evil. Wind lifted the tips of fallen banners and whistled through the jagged stones still standing on the wall.

When the guards of Edlad made their first rounds of the area, they discovered that Wictred's footprints (which were distinct because his feet were deformed, cloven like a goat's feet) could be found leading right up to the wall, the border of the city, but apparently that is as far as he got. He never set foot inside the city walls.

As they contemplated this, they heard a stirring and rustling coming from somewhere right outside the wall.

"Woof, woof!" came the sound.

"Why you old fleabag, where you been all this time?" said an old man to his dog.

Cnebba, blood stained and stuck with several arrows, was in this manner found to be still alive.

Chapter 18
The Miracle on the Wall

The King was not aware of any of this, for he had laid his daughter upon her bed and sat beside her. However, Erinndis did feel upon her lips the cool taste of the dew that came from above, and it kept her from dying right away. But she was not healed of her malady and her bones were still broken from her fall. The King sat beside his daughter for about two hours, until evening.

About an hour after sunset, Adrastos came in to see the King and his daughter.

"Come, my king. There is one last, great task for the Emerald of Healing to perform. Carry your daughter as gently as you can and come," said the priest.

The King followed the priest with his daughter

in his arms. They were now joined by a company of lesser priests and knights that had fought in the last battle. The procession walked slowly through the Great Hall and out of the castle door. They walked through the Orchard, now dark, and finally through a colonnade of arches that led from the Orchard into the camps for the refugees.

As they passed under the arches they saw a multitude of people bearing torches, waiting for them at Adrastos' command. Many who were healed of the plague and many who had been hungry stood and watched as King Athelgar carried their Queen, his daughter, up a flight of stairs on the wall that led to a slab of black rock on the top of the wall. Aldhelm and Frealaf were among them.

Finally, the King reached the top of the steps; and he stood facing the slab, his back toward his people, for a good moment. Adrastos had placed the Emerald on a table just behind and above the slab. Then, he gently placed his daughter on her feet, standing her up at foot of the slab.

"Stand, my daughter," he said. The Emerald glowed brightly, but this time all it enabled her to do was to wince when she struggled to rise. King Athelgar slowly backed off, leaving his daughter to face the slab alone. The slab was raised about one cubit above the surrounding area, and Erinndis turned to face the people and placed her calves upon the edge of the slab.

She remained standing silently, till all eyes were upon her. Suddenly, the Emerald shone forth with a light from beyond the world, not blinding, yet bright as seven suns; beautiful like the light of a thousand spring flowers on a calm morning. Erinndis' arms shot up toward heaven as if in worship. The people gasped. Then, as the light from the Emerald faded, she turned her palms slightly inward as if to grip invisible hands; and slowly, slowly, she bent backwards, down toward the black stone. The people gasped again . . . for her feet came out from under her, but instead of falling, behold! She descended as gently as a bubble through still air.

As the people wondered at this, a cloudy pink light began to pool like water around the base of the stone slab. Then, the light fluttered and began to rise, finally enveloping the entire slab. The Queen sunk into the pink light as if into a feather bed, and it slowly closed over her with a soft splash. The whole thing resembled a pool of glowing pinkish-red water suspended in the air, as it were, with the base of the stone table forming the base of a tank whose sides were invisible. As the pink light began to darken, red shapes from within seemed to dance inside of it. Darkening further, the whole mass formed itself into a - - what was it exactly? Some thought it resembled a wooden coffin. Others thought it looked more like the cocoon of a butterfly in the springtime.

Suddenly, white light exploded outward from the coffin in a blinding flash that lit up the clouds against the black sky. At that very moment the pain in Aldhelm's right arm vanished.

As the people regained their night vision, they were treated to a sight even more stunning. Where once there had been a hard stony slab, there now rested a sumptuous feather bed, bathed in a cool pink glow. A beautiful girl, with flowing golden hair, rose slowly from the soft bed. She rubbed sleep from her eyes and yawned. A hush of wonder was upon the crowd, as her beauty was so great that the yawn alone evoked distant memories of lost youth, of first loves, in the good people of the kingdom who had gathered on this night. As she stood and walked along the wall, the people's eyes were fastened tightly upon the winsome girl.

Aldhelm gasped. Was that not the same girl he had met in the moonlight not so long ago? And she was even more beautiful now than she was then.

There now rested a golden glow on top of the wall (where the slab had been) that bathed the surrounding areas in a sweet light. An aerial display of blue, pink and white doves exploded out of that central light, spread, and then danced around the tops of the highest parapets of the castle. Immediately after this the glowing doves dissolved into gold and silver sparks that showered the people watching below.

Suddenly there appeared a light in the sky . . . bright as the sun, some thought; and though it dazzled, it didn't blind anyone. As eyes got used to the light they could see that it was made of a shimmering stairway like glittering diamonds that led from the top of the wall up into a doorway in heaven. No details could be seen through the doorway, but dancing lights seemed to move to and fro in it.

Erinndis, who was now glowing white, looked back at the people for a moment, and then began to ascend the stairs. As she got closer to the doorway the vision faded, and the stairway was no longer bright as the sun but now like the moon, and finally like a wispy trail of stardust.

Aldhelm's heart now sank, for he knew that he could not rise into the heavens with his love, again found, and again lost. He sunk to one knee and bowed his head.

So spectacular was this sight, the people had not noticed that King Athelgar and Adrastos the priest had gone down the steps, reformed the procession, and walked back into the castle.

They also had not noticed that the Emerald was gone.

Chapter 19
An End and a Beginning

The next night, king Athelgar began grieving for Erinndis. He was grieved that she would no longer be with him, but his grief was tempered by the fact that she had been taken, as it were, to a better place. And he had been able to see her completely healed, and able to see her go, with his own eyes. He had peered into a land beyond or above our own, and his heart, always hopeful, was greatly reassured by this vision.

"What really happened up there? Did my daughter really die? If not, where did she go?" the king asked Adrastos during this time.

"She was translated to the Celestial Gardens, close to the domain of the Great King. It is the realm from which good dreams originate if they do not come from heaven itself. At certain times no one on earth can predict, doors to this realm have been known to open.

You might see your daughter again before your earthly days are finished, but no one can say when or where."

Athelgar's heart was greatly comforted by these words, and after about a week he stopped grieving for Erinndis.

When the time of grieving was over came the great feast of victory, mandatory for all the kings of Kara Mundalyn whenever they won a war. Torches lit the great hall and, as was traditional, the king led the procession of important guests to the tables. Toasts and speeches were given, and roast beef was served. The minstrels in the gallery bathed the hall in joyful song and everyone ate.

"Why did we not hear from you all these years?" said Lord Sigeric between bites.

"Believe me, I tried to get word to you many times. Toward the end I understand that we were partially successful, though my missive wasn't in nearly as good shape when it arrived as it was when it left my hand," said King Athelgar.

"Are we to hear more details in meetings to come?" offered Heorogar.

"The time to tell the full tale will indeed come," said Athelgar. "But I can tell you some of it now. We were led into a very cleverly designed trap outside of Snagov, in the Mountains of the Giants. Our goal was to seal the Tomb of the Ghoul, and to do that we had to destroy the army of the Giant King. But when we arrived, the engineers of Snagov set off an avalanche of rocks that sealed us in valley ringed with cliffs.

I also believe that there was some kind of spell, because as long as we were in the shadow of the Black Crag, our efforts were greatly hindered in many strange ways.

I think they intended for us to lose hope in that trap. But though several years passed, our courage did not fail. We found water and eventually were able to grow our own food. So successful were our efforts that as time went by we even began taking in new recruits, some of which came back with us and fought in the battle of Edlad. During this time we defeated the Giants and sealed the tomb of the Ghoul, a hole from which many foul things had been emerging from beneath the earth.

Then our own engineers began preparing to remove the wall of rocks that kept us trapped, and they would have done it in about six months, but the men of Snagov surprised us by breaking down their own wall. To finish us off, perhaps? We were quite ready for them and after destroying that army we left the valley and came home."

"And we were very glad to see you indeed!" said several of those seated.

These festivities were over when Adrastos came up to talk to the King. The priest had decided that men were never meant to be the stewards of the jewels of healing. The remaining jewels of healing had to be returned to the mountains. They should be left where God put them, hidden; their powers being tapped only when He wills, not when man wills.

"The great Emerald has given itself so that the Queen might be saved," said the priest. "Now I must give myself so that the kingdom might be saved. I will take the jewels up the Great Mountain myself. I will take them to the heights where men cannot breathe. I will ascend to these heights by breaking the ancient law which says, 'Do not use the gems to preserve your own life where nature decrees that it should end.' Then I will bury all the gems in the mountain."

He paused.

"I will not be coming back," said Adrastos.

"No!" came a chorus of voices.

"My friends, my time is over," he said softly and gently. "The priesthood of the North has failed, and I am ultimately responsible. Skaldar, one of the most trusted of our order, has betrayed the secrets of the gems of healing to the most evil king on earth. I myself trusted him completely."

Then he spoke in a louder and more commanding voice.

"Never again can any man be trusted with the healing gems, no, not even priests. Monsters like Wictred will rise again, and the temptation to use the great power of the healing jewels for evil will eventually overcome any precautions we can take, unless we put them forever out of the reach of man," he said.

"I think this is folly," said King Athelgar. "Once something becomes known to men, it cannot be

154

permanently hidden again, no matter how great the precaution. Do not throw away your life like this. I forbid it."

"But you know the law, my King. A priest who sacrifices his own life in order to save the lives of others cannot be prevented from doing so, not even by the king. You cannot lawfully prevent me from going," said Adrastos.

"You are right about the law," said the king. "However, the law also specifies that the priest may give his life only if it is clear that he will save another . . . and I think that is far from clear. Perhaps the lives that would be saved by keeping the gems are more than those that would be saved by disposing of them. Remember also that the gems only heal the righteous."

Lord Sigeric put down his wine and said, "How then was Wictred healed of his deadly wound in the battle?"

Adrastos begin to reply, ""I believe he found a way to bend the power of the jewels to his will . . . all the more reason why I must take the jewels . . ."

"The priests shall guard the gems as before!" shouted Athelgar in a loud voice. "The priesthood has now been purged of evil . . . Skaldar is gone."

Then, turning to Adrastos, he said "I absolutely forbid you to do this thing, and I will hear no more of it."

. . .

Several days after Heorogar and his men had charged up Mount Hope, they came back down the ledge without king Wictred.

"We followed him as far as we could, but he kept going. The air got thinner and thinner, and we slowed down. Finally, his dead horse came rolling down at us and nearly knocked one of our knights off of the path. He had run it to death. Somehow he kept going on foot, faster than our horses could carry us. By some magic he ran past the Face in the Rock, and we lost sight of him in the heights. We have posted a guard to make sure that he never comes down, even if by his sorceries he survives for a while. If he returns we will capture him," said Heorogar to the King.

"I did not know that the Gthonic king had such a rugged constitution that he could outrun even the noble Heorogar," said the King. "If I had known that, I would have taken my own knights and pursued him myself, for in the shadow of the Black Crag we were forced to fight in the cold air heights. I now realize that one must train in the high mountains in order to fight in the high mountains.

I therefore decree that a wall shall be built to block the ledge. It shall be built as high as it can be built, where the lungs of the workers shall be near bursting. There we will train our young knights to fight and endure on the mountain heights.

"Evil was last seen fleeing upon that ledge. The wall shall be a testimony to all that it shall not return. The wall will stand in the sight of Edlad, so that all may look up at it and know that we stood against evil. They will say to evil, 'that way you went, and from thence you shall not return, for we shall stand against you.'"

Adrastos then said, "I too would like to see this wall built. May the day come when we can stand here together and behold the wall gleaming in the bright sun."

Adrastos had always been truthful, so King Athelgar, who feared Adrastos might still try to leave, rested a little easier, for now he could now delay the completion of the wall's construction for a long time, though his knights began training that very day.

. . .

The kingdom had lost its beloved princess and its Emerald, but it had regained its king.

Without the threat from the East, the king had a free hand to institute many changes. The sorceress under the mountain packed up her things and moved through the Great Mountains out into lands beyond . . . the chronicles do not record where. She did not want to live under Athelgar's new laws.

No one knows how she got through those mountains, but either the powers that dwelt there did not mind evil *leaving* the kingdom, or else she had some magic to make herself invisible to them. Eadward, who was so interested in the dark arts, was never seen again after the battle.

Eadwacer the moneylender, having repented earlier, now also confessed to having cheated Cnebba. He paid him back double, and did the same to anyone else he had cheated. Since Cnebba was now highly regarded in the kingdom, this went a good way toward softening the people's anger toward the moneylender.

Eadwacer renounced all his claims on other people's lands, and spent the rest of his money traveling about the kingdom doing good deeds. His son Eadgils had difficulty learning to live without a talisman, but he was determined to succeed, and eventually he did.

Anlaf and Forthred returned to the forest with a lucrative contract to supply the King's carpenters with wood, and they became very rich. Gudlaug no longer dug her own garden, but she commanded several dozen gardeners who grew fruits that became famous throughout the land for their sweetness and flowers famed for their beauty. The families enjoyed several prosperous and happy years with their growing sons.

Frealaf received the medal of honor for his stand against the Gthonic king. He later became one of Athelgar's greatest knights.

Aldhelm eventually became one of the great explorers in the Kingdom, mapping out those areas that had been blank spaces on older maps. Often he traveled beyond the mountains, and his adventures are recorded in the chronicles of Kara Mundalyn. Aldhelm held to the hope that somehow, some way, he would again meet his beloved.

Odanae's drawings and plans for buildings impressed the King, and he began to study to become an architect. In the years to come he would grow into a great builder and be commissioned to build a new city in the West, which would be named after King Athelgar.

Uncle Cnebba had a new job also. He was now the second chief of the Guards, reporting to Healfdene. Often he could be seen walking in and around the castle grounds with his faithful companion Burgleburper, who had saved the Emerald and in so doing saved Erinndis for a better life. People said that as long as those two were on the job, no evil could ever touch the castle.

And so it was that the battle of Edlad was not the twilight of Kara Mundalyn. It was just a bad midday storm, and the kingdom would enjoy a long sunny afternoon of peace and prosperity that surpassed its morning time.

No dark shadows plagued the kingdom for many years, and when children did have nightmares, they called out to the Most High King, whose dwelling is not with men; and a stream of light would trickle down from heaven, and a blanket of light would cover the child, and the shadows would howl and hide, for the light was stronger than the darkness.

The end.

www.ingramcontent.com/pod-product-compliance
Lightning Source LLC
Chambersburg PA
CBHW020730210626
46807CB00016B/1131